Praise for Alma M

I loved the story. It truly captured Alma, her so revealing interactions and thoughts, and all the while with sly humor. I enjoy reading complex characters, and this story builds to an inspired ending.

I got hooked on this character, empathized with her and even got mad at her. Her evolving spirit and the twists and turns of her unusual life were a delight to read.

The dialogue is so good, many times I heard the conversations in my head.

Glad I could read this.

- Denise Dion Ph.D., Psychologist

Alma has problems. Or perhaps more accurately, Alma has *no* problems - at least none of the sort that would send her into a tailspin. No, Alma doesn't do tailspins. And *that*, it would seem - is a problem.

As our narrator leads us through the labyrinth of Alma's life, through the ups and downs that might drive a lesser woman to drink, we feel the regrets that Alma cannot feel and the joys that elude her. And because she lives in no small part in each of us, our storyteller's compassionate perspective soothes our mutual wounds. His fascination with Alma becomes ours and his analysis informs our own private therapy.

Doug Puryear's Alma is a woman whose story resounds with the effects of a difficult childhood - not uncommon these days. But far from being a tragedy, it's a story that speaks to the development of personality and the innate ingenuity that enables humans to adapt and go on. And though Alma is not normal -

whatever that is, her story suggests that sometimes we might all wish to be so crazy.

- Chris Thomas BA, MA, is a scriptwriter, winner of multiple awards and competitions. She has been involved with the Boulder Writing Studio in Boulder, Colorado.

I thoroughly enjoyed reading Alma Means Soul. The dialogue consists primarily of simple declarative sentences-without the stylistic flourishes and arcane verbiage which to me diminish the joy of reading. On another level the novel tells an important but frequently overlooked American success story. We have become obsessed with the grand success stories primarily in technology and finance - Jamie Dimon, Bill Gates, Mark Zuckerberg, etc. Untold are the stories of the strivers from impoverished and abusive childhoods pursuing less lofty goals. The story of Alma and her dress shop could be replicated by stories of strivers from similar backgrounds opening bodegas, Halal stands, Small Chinese eateries, pizzerias, etc.

This novel is a great read and speaks to deeper trends in American society.

- Victor Whitman, MD, Pediatric Cardiologist

ALMA MEANS SOUL

A Novel

Douglas A. Puryear

Disclaimer: This is a work of fiction. Any resemblance to any person, place, thing or situation, living or dead, present or past, is purely coincidental.

Is this true?

These characters live in my head. They may contain portions of people and experiences I've experienced or read about or heard of. Where they do, the characters are composites of various people, including at times myself, stitched together somewhat like Frankenstein's monster, but, I hope, more attractive. Well, most of them.

Doug Puryear

©, 2019 by Douglas A. Puryear. All rights reserved.

ISBN-13: 9798507657209

To Martha, of course, love you more.

Other Books by Doug Puryear

Non-fiction:

Helping People in Crisis

Your Life Can Be Better, using strategies for adult ADHD, Second Edition

Living Daily with Adult ADHD, 365 Tips O the Day

The Bully

It's Been A Great Ride: with some bumps

Fiction:

Just this one, so far.

ALMA MEANS SOUL

PRE PRELUDE

I never met the lady and I regret that. I only saw her once, at a distance. It was back when I was young and healthy, at a cocktail party, and I learned a little bit about her there. Then I forgot her, or I thought I had. But years later, I got an update on her and I remembered her. After that, she was quietly stuck in my mind.

I don't know why she had such a hold on me, maybe because her problems and personality were similar to my own? Or maybe just because the trajectory of her life caught my interest. Eventually I realized she'd stay with me until I got her story told.

Maybe she'd been there all along.

PRELUDE

AT THE FACULTY PARTY

She wasn't bad looking. Really not bad looking at all, especially for a woman her age, late forties? Maybe early fifties. Didn't look like she'd had any face work done; that's a turn off for me. And she looked like she was rich, which is why I asked my wife if she knew anything about her. I've always been interested in rich women. My wife wasn't rich when I married her and she wasn't rich now, the small income from my novels not adding much to the salary of a professor in a small college, a small salary even though I was teaching both English Lit and science, which should've counted for something extra, but didn't. And so my wife still wouldn't be rich after I was gone, unless she got lucky. She disliked me telling her how much I hoped I went first.

My wife looked at me suspiciously. "Why? Why are you asking about her?"

"Just curious."

"It wouldn't have anything to do with her being good looking, would it?"

"Well, that doesn't hurt. But I was just curious."

"OK. Well, maybe I'll tell you then."

During the time my wife was gathering her thoughts, or whatever the hell it is women do at a time like that, my mind drifted back to my quesadilla. Quesadillas to be honest. I make them myself and they're wonderfully good and I never stop at just one. My secret is using at least three different kinds of cheese, a lot of onion and a lot of salt. But what the hell was that black thing I nearly broke my tooth on this morning and how the hell did it get into my quesadilla, which I'd just made myself with my own two loving hands? I'd come to a dead end on that question when my wife spoke.

"Hmmm," she said. "Tell you what. You go get me a nice glass of wine and I'll tell you what I know."

"White or red ?"

"You choose," she answered.

That's unusual, because one thing you can say about my wife is she knows her own mind. It suggested she was really mulling over the story.

I got her a glass of Pinot Noir and myself a beer, in the bottle so I could sip it slowly, and I over tipped the young bar girl who had favored me with a nice smile like I was a real person and not just another jerk. Besides, I didn't have the right denomination and it would've looked cheap to ask her for change. And besides, she was good looking. She said, "Thank you," smiling again, and "Be seeing you."

I smiled, nodded, and moved off, trying not to spill any of my wife's Pinot, of which the girl had poured a generous portion. I knew the smile and the words meant nothing except that she was working for tips and maybe I reminded her of her grandfather, but still -.

My wife sniffed the Pinot. "Nice," she said, taking a sip. "You sure know how to show a girl a good time. OK, here's what I know."

It turns out the lady in question had been married to my wife's second cousin, Ed. I've never been good at these things, but I guess that makes me her ex second cousin once removed in law or something like that. Or it did make me that. My wife informed me that Ed's dead now. Then she started telling the not bad looking lady's story.

DADDY'S COMING HOME

"Mary Alma! Mary Alma!"

Mary Alma heard the tension in her mother's voice; she didn't have to look at the clock to know what time it was, Daddy's coming home time. She trudged slowly into the kitchen where her mother stood waiting, wine glass in hand.

"It's about time you showed up. Get the kids into the basement, quick. No noise now."

She didn't need to say any of that, because Mary Alma knew the drill.

So Mary Alma, at eight years the oldest of the four children, herded them into the basement where they pretended to play board games while listening intently to the sounds from upstairs. If they didn't hear the front door slamming followed by their father's yelling and cursing, it was gonna be a good evening and they could go upstairs and greet him with a kiss and a hug, given willingly, for the most part.

And they never heard their mother's whimpers. Mary Alma had learned early not to creep to the top of the stairs and listen, for her mother's whimpers were heartbreaking and in fact, more frightening than their father's yelling. If it was one of the bad evenings, they'd have to wait downstairs until it got quiet and then they could tiptoe up the stairs, careful not to wake up their father dozing in the big armchair in front of the TV tuned to nothing in particular, with a last drink near his hand, unless he'd spilled it.

No outsiders knew what was going on in the house although some astute teachers might've guessed something. The children instinctively knew never to speak of it to anyone and they never invited friends over after school. And their mother was able to do magic with a little makeup, as she should have been since she worked in a beauty parlor, even though her specialty was hair, not makeup.

And Mary Alma's mother wasn't an alcoholic, as she'd explained to Mary Alma many times, because she only drank white wine and had never gotten any of the DWI's the father collected, nor tumbled down the basement stairs as the father once had to the terror of the children below, nor gotten violent, not ever.

What effect did all of this have on Mary Alma? It caused her to be very wary. And to vow that when she grew up she'd have a lotta money so she'd be totally independent and not trapped as her mother apparently was. And to vow that she'd never get involved with a man, although she was already somewhat ambivalent about that.

And nothing in her childhood experiences changed her mind in the least about either vow, not until she hit puberty anyway.

There were other effects, too, which Mary Alma could never have articulated because she was unaware of them.

Mary Alma's father was an in-town truck driver, a delivery man. He knew the town backwards and forwards and upside down, too, sober or not quite sober. He was so good that whenever he was fired for not showing up or for messing up a delivery, some other business hired him right away. The taxi companies even occasionally hired him to train their new drivers, until later when he got sloppy and unreliable; he'd made a decent living for his family up until then. He loved his children and he was actually a nice man when he was sober. But as an adult, Mary Alma would remember the bad nights as almost every night. In reality they averaged one or two nights a week and occasionally a whole week went by without any unpleasantness. There were enough good times that his children loved him; they alternated between love and terror. But memory is a tricky thing and cannot be relied on.

Her mother was, well, her mother. And she only drank white wine.

Mary Alma's father never talked about the war. On the few occasions when one of the children asked him, his face would freeze; he'd give them a cold stare and say, "That's all over and done with now." The angry set of his mouth suggested they'd best not ask him again. Once though Mary Alma persisted. "Yes, I know, but what did you do?" He glared at her and raised his hand and she thought he was going to hit her, but he dropped his hand, turned and walked off. The door banged shut and then she heard the truck roar off and when he returned several hours later he was drunk.

Mary Alma remembered little about her father from before he went off to war, shortly after her brother was born. She did remember his coming home for a short while which she later learned was a two-week furlough. When he left again, her mother cried, which was a rare thing, at least in front of the children. Before the furlough, their mother used to read his letters to Mary Alma and her brother, but afterwards, she didn't anymore.

Mary Alma also remembered her father's brother coming to visit before her father left the second time. She didn't remember the brother himself but that he brought them presents and he was wearing a uniform and driving a car like she'd never seen before, a long station wagon with genuine wood on the sides.

Sometimes Mary Alma learned things by listening to the adults when they weren't aware of her presence or when she pretended she wasn't listening. She was good at that.

After the war was over, when Mary Alma was seven and her father came home for good, she learned that his brother had been killed.

Mary Alma's father didn't like swimming and the few times he went he was the only man who kept his shirt on. One day she passed her parent's bedroom and saw him standing with his back to a mirror, looking over his shoulder at the ugly red jagged scar that ran from his right shoulder nearly to his hip. He noticed her standing there staring and walked over and shut the door. That was the only time she ever saw him without a shirt on.

Mary Alma and her little brother explored the back of the hall closet and found a trunk covered with a blanket. They drug it out of the closet and inside they found a pistol, a uniform, some letters tied with a string which they left alone, and two photos. In one photo a lot of men in uniform stood stiffly in rows. She assumed one was her father although she couldn't pick him out. In the other her father and two other men in uniform held rifles. They looked very young and they were smiling.

The children were guessing which man in the big picture was their father when he came down the hall. He didn't say a word, just shoved the trunk back into the closet and slammed the door. Mary Alma and her brother were paralyzed, wide eyed and trembling. Their father stood glaring at them until Mary Alma suddenly turned and ran and her brother raced after her. She and her brother never talked about this and her father never mentioned it.

The trunk was gone when Mary Alma peeked into the closet a week later. For a long time she remembered how scared she'd been and the picture of the men with the rifles. She had a nightmare about it one night.

Like the war, her father would never discuss his parents; he'd just say, "Not now," or occasionally, "None of your business," but Mary Alma did learn they lived far away. She never met them or heard anything from them. One died when she was six and the other when she was eleven. They'd been gone for weeks before she heard about it.

Her mother's parents were a mystery, too. Whenever her mother was asked about them, the answer was, "They've been dead a long time now so there's no use talking about them."

Mary Alma didn't realize any of this was strange until she was an adult but she knew other children had grandparents and aunts and uncles and sometimes she thought that she and her siblings could use a few of those.

After Mary Alma was grown and out of the house, in one of her infrequent phone conversations with her mother she asked why there'd never been any contact with her father's parents. Her mother sighed and said, "They just weren't interested in us." She paused, then added, "They had their own problems. And you remember my parents were gone before you were even born." She would say no more and she never would answer even the simple question of where any of the grandparents were from.

It would be many years before Mary Alma learned anything about any of her grandparents or the reasons for all the secrecy.

Mary Alma's mother went to church sometimes, Our Lady of Perpetual Something or Other. Mary Alma was baptized there. When she was nine, Mary Alma attended a few confirmation classes. The teacher was an old strict retired school teacher who disapproved of questions. She wore a high necked blouse and a long skirt, with a heavy black cross around her neck and a big black belt that seemed like a threat.

Mary Alma easily memorized the dogmas in her Catholic catechism book. She saw that the teacher spent a lot of time off track, pushing her own dogmas about the sins of abortion, divorce, sex in general and especially the sin which she couldn't speak and called "That other stuff." It took Mary Alma a while to figure out what that meant.

The class bored Mary Alma and she didn't like the teacher. She quit going. Mary Alma's mother was enmeshed in the drama with the father and she lacked the energy to push Mary Alma on the issue. Besides, she needed Mary Alma at home to help with the younger three. But confirmation class helped Mary Alma figure out why her mother didn't leave her father, although she didn't understand all the reasons. Of course, she never asked her mother about it.

THE MOVIE: TOO MUCH, TOO SOON FOR MARY ALMA

When Mary Alma was five, one of her mother's church friends, fulfilling her Christian duty of charity, took Mary Alma to a movie, Walt Disney's Fantasia. In a strange place, alone in the dark with a stranger, blaring music shaking her seat and glaring colors hurting her eyes, Mary Alma's sobs could not be restrained.

The woman's "Hush!"s and shoulder pats didn't calm her and they rushed out. "You ungrateful child! I do something nice for you and you ruin it. I was enjoying the movie. I'll never do anything for you again, you can count on that!" That was fine with Mary Alma.

The woman dragged Mary Alma through her front door by a painful grip on her arm. She described the child's outrageous behavior to the mother and stormed out with a snort while the mother was still apologizing.

Her mother wasn't happy. "What's wrong with you? That's a movie for kids. Kids love it. Why'd you make a scene? And quit sniffling."

At five years old, Mary Alma couldn't explain beyond, "I didn't like it. I didn't like it." This didn't satisfy her mother and she sent Mary Alma to her room for the rest of the day, but later she relented and called the child back to set the table. She relented, but she gave the cold shoulder until the next day. The incident was mentioned only a couple of more times and then it was forgotten as other events unfolded.

THE ACCIDENT: MARY ALMA'S SKINNED KNEE

Mary Alma rode her bike to and from school. This was considered safe back then, and besides, her parents had things on their minds other than her safety.

When she was nine years old, riding home from school, Mary Alma skidded on a patch of ice and crashed. She tore her pants leg and skinned her knee and her bicycle front wheel was bent. She walked the bike home and held her tears in until she got to the kitchen. Then she broke into sobs when she saw her mother. It did hurt, after all, and the crash had scared her.

"What happened?" her mother exclaimed, and before she could answer, "Now stop that crying. You're not a baby."

"It hurts," Mary Alma sobbed.

"It's nothing," her mother said. "Grow up. Quit crying, you'll upset the other kids and I don't have time to fool with them. Go get the iodine out of the bathroom."

Mary Alma stopped crying. "No," she said, "I'll be OK."

"Go get the iodine. The last thing I need is for you to get an infection and I'll have to take you to the doctor and buy medicine and all that. Go on now."

Mary Alma had never had iodine applied but she'd seen its effect on the younger kids and she assumed it must hurt like a booger. But she went and got it. She handed the iodine to her mother who set her wine glass down and actually looked at the knee. Or at the pants leg anyway.

"Oh, my. Look what you've done. I'll have to mend those, and I'm not sure I can get the blood out. OK, now be still and I'll put this on your knee and I don't want to hear another peep out of you. I don't have time for this nonsense."

Mary Alma wondered what it was that had her mother so busy. From what she could see, all her mother had been doing was sitting at the kitchen counter watching a soap opera on the small black and white kitchen TV, but of course, she didn't say anything. Mary Alma pulled her pants down to her ankles and sat in a chair facing her mother. She bit her lip when the iodine was applied. It hurt, but not as much as she'd expected, and she didn't make a sound.

Her mother closed the bottle and said, "Now put this back where it belongs and leave your pants on the floor. I'll get to them when I can."

She refilled her wine glass and turned back to the TV.

And that was that.

Except when Mary Alma's father got home, he was relatively sober and he saw the damaged bike on the front porch. He exploded. "Are you an idiot? How in the hell did you manage to do that? Don't you know those things cost money?"

Mary Alma just stared at the floor. Her father stopped ranting and stomped to his easy chair, mumbling all the way. Mary Alma went to the kid's bedroom and closed the door. She had a few sobs left but she kept them quiet and started on her homework. which wasn't interesting but kept her mind off the pain in her knee and anything else that might have been bothering her.

The next day her father did a great job of fixing her bike, making it nearly as good as new, except for some paint scratched off the front fender, and he didn't bother with that. The accident was never mentioned again and Mary Alma's knee healed quickly with no problem, although there was a small scar left. On her knee, I mean. Maybe that wasn't the only scar?

MARY ALMA AND HER THREE, NO, TWO SIBLINGS

Mary Alma's brother died from the measles when he was nine. The youngest girl got measles, too, but she wasn't so sick. He was though; he had a high fever. Their mother kept putting cold cloths on him and had Mary Alma wringing them out and bringing her fresh pans of cold water and then he had a convulsion and then he died.

You may wonder if the boy had had his vaccinations. Well, no, he hadn't. Mary Alma had been vaccinated, but not the younger children; the mother said she was just too busy. When they started school, it was easier to claim religious objections. But none of that's relevant here, because the measles vaccine wasn't available until years after the boy's death. So, although after a death we tend to look for somebody to blame, we can't blame this one on the mother.

The mother was distraught of course and wept a lot for a couple of weeks, but Mary Alma had little feeling about it. She certainly didn't miss the boy. She'd taken care of him, practically raised him, and he was just an average kid, not any particular trouble, but she'd never felt any real connection to him. She didn't go to the funeral but stayed home and looked after the girls. The father didn't attend because he'd left the house when the boy died and didn't return for four days. This had never happened before.

But soon all was the same as before except for a little more white wine and more frequent bad nights and Mary Alma had one less child to look after, and that was that.

Years later, when Mary Alma was eighteen, her next younger sister got pregnant. At fourteen. Her father cursed her, then beat her and kicked her out of the house. The mother's mild objections had no effect. The girl moved in with her boyfriend's family, who were nicer to her. The baby was adopted. The sister moved to another state, lied about her age, and got an office job in a trucking company. She married but kept working and she never had another child. She divorced, remarried, divorced again. For eight or nine years after Mary Alma left home, she and her sister exchanged Christmas cards or occasionally had a phone call, always uncomfortable for Mary Alma although she never shared much. Then the calls stopped and the cards became occasional. Then the sisters lost touch. Mary Alma thought this strange and hoped nothing was wrong, but she didn't worry about it.

Mary Alma had more attachment to her youngest sister, who she called "Two," although attachment may be too strong a word. When they were grown they never wrote, not even Christmas cards, but kept in touch with infrequent phone calls, which were meaningful for Two, who thought her big sister a sympathetic listener. They were less important to Mary Alma, who contributed little to the conversations but felt some value in keeping in touch, occasional though it was but enough for her.

Mary Alma had never wondered about her name but one Saturday morning her mother, after her second glass of white wine, was leaning against the kitchen counter watching Mary Alma wash the breakfast dishes and put them in the rack to dry. Out of the blue, her mother asked, "Did I ever tell you where your name came from?"

Mary Alma was concentrating on the dishes. She'd learned the hard way that not breaking any was more important than getting them clean although she was careful about that, too, because she knew about germs from school.

She really wasn't interested and didn't respond.

"Well, I'll tell you. Mary, of course, is for our Blessed Virgin, and Alma because it was my Grandma's name. We called her Nessie, but her name was Alma. Did I ever tell you about her?"

Mary Alma shook her head no and continued with the dishes.

"She was sweet, old and shriveled up, but nice to me. She always had a piece of candy hidden away for me. She'd tell me not to let anybody else know about it because then everybody would want some.

Do you know what Alma means?"

Mary Alma shook her head again.

"Well, it's Spanish and my Grandma was a little bit Spanish and it means soul, and so that's what I named you, Mary Alma."

Mary Alma had finished the dishes and she hung the dishrag up to dry. "OK," she said, and when she turned from the sink she was surprised to see tears in her mother's eyes.

"Sometimes, somehow, you remind me of her," her mother said.

But Mary Alma had already left the room.

In high school, Mary Alma decided Mary was too commonplace and she would go by her middle name. She was insistent about this and soon everyone, except her mother, was calling her Alma.

I guess this change indicates some maturing and some independence. And there would be more change, including some slippage of one of her two vows.

HERE'S ED

Alma was a B and C student; she was bright but none of her subjects were interesting nor her teachers inspiring. Senior year she had her first date, and she dated Ed for a while. He wasn't very interesting or inspiring either, but he was on the football team, a cut above the band, chorus, or debate club. Ed wasn't very good and he didn't get to play much.

Ed played end. He wasn't fast and didn't have good hands, but he was a fairly good blocker or he would've been on the fourth string instead of the third, if there'd been a fourth string. Well, not actually a fairly good blocker, but he'd developed an illegal technique of holding that was hard to detect and he never got a penalty for it. Once in practice a teammate he was holding got frustrated and punched him in the stomach. Ed was so astonished that his only response was exclaiming, "What the shit?!"

The assistant coach saw the exchange and asked what was going on. The teammate exclaimed, "He's been holding me every damn time!"

The coach said, "Tough cookies!" and then the next play was called and Ed kept holding because that's all he knew how to do.

Ed didn't like football but he was trying to please his daddy.

It didn't work.

Ed's daddy owned the third largest used car lot in town and was fairly successful. Some said this was because he wasn't hampered by an overdeveloped sense of honesty. Still, he'd never been caught cheating on Ed's mama, his second wife.

For some reason, Ed's daddy never liked Ed. He never abused him, just was mostly indifferent. He was a sports fan but although Ed kept at football throughout high school, his daddy only went to a few of the games.

Ed's daddy was an introvert. That may be part of why he wasn't involved with Ed. Part. But you wouldn't know anything about his shyness while he was selling you a used car. Then he was the friendliest, most jovial, and funniest guy you'd ever want to meet. Just don't try to bring the car back if it turned out to be a lemon.

Alma broke up with Ed a few months after football season ended. He wasn't very interesting, the status was gone and he was too pushy about sex regardless of how she felt. And she was busy taking care of her sisters. She decided on the direct approach for the breakup. Ed drove up out front one evening. He never honked, not after the first time when she'd straightened him out about that, so he just waited. Alma came out to the car but she didn't open the door, just leaned in the window.

"Ed, I don't want to go out with you anymore."

Ed was silent for a moment. Then he turned the key in the ignition and without looking at her said, "OK," and sped off. And that was that.

Well, not quite.

Shortly before graduation Alma told Ed she was pregnant. He looked at her, sucked in a long breath, and said, "Are you sure it's mine?"

She slapped him, hard.

Ed's response was the same as when the teammate slugged him. The deer in the headlights startled stare and then, "What the shit?!"

I wouldn't assume Ed's go-to response was any clue to his intelligence or his emotional maturity, but I wouldn't assume it wasn't either.

They waited to get married until after graduation, which neither attended.

The wedding wasn't fancy but a lot of the high school kids came, for the drinks at the reception. The reception was a flop. The booze ran out and the caterer got lost on the way and by the time she arrived half the guests had left for more promising venues and the food was cold. It was a sad little affair.

Ed and Alma left on their honeymoon soon after the caterer arrived. Alma skipped the bouquet tossing. She drove because Ed was so drunk he couldn't make it to the car without help. She also checked them into the cheap motel where they'd made reservations, entirely unnecessary. Ed made it to the bathroom before he barfed. Alma made him sleep on the floor. He didn't care.

Two months later Alma miscarried. Neither Alma nor Ed were particularly unhappy about that. I might think it a blessing, considering the circumstances, but Alma wouldn't have used that term; she didn't think that way.

Alma and Ed limped along in their marriage for a while. Ed enrolled at the community college but his heart wasn't in college any more than it had been in football. He spent a lot of time out drinking with old high school buddies, about the only thing he had any real talent for. He'd made no friends at college, where most of the students were older, employed, and more serious about education than about drinking. Alma largely ignored him, although they slept in the same bed and occasionally were what tends to be called "intimate," not satisfying to either of them, but it was a release.

Ed's daddy was supporting them although Alma worked part-time in a woman's dress shop and tried to sell Tupperware. She also dawdled through one course at the school Ed attended.

Attended is probably the right word because Ed wasn't setting the school afire scholastically, barely managing passing grades. There were several possible ways to achieve this, and it was important because his daddy's support depended on Ed's being in school.

Ed and Alma got a dog. Maybe they were thinking that a dog could somehow improve their marriage although Alma wasn't optimistic about that. But Ed had always had a dog and he insisted they get one. Maybe it was a macho thing, too.

They rescued a moderately large mixed breed from the pound. They'd agreed that mongrels were better than purebreds; of course, they couldn't have afforded a purebred even if they'd wanted one. Later they agreed that this particular mongrel had turned out to be especially stupid and that he could produce an impressive amount of poop for his size. They didn't agree on much else.

"Ed! Hey, Ed!"

Alma was calling from the other end of the house.

"Yo! What is it?"

"Come here. I can't talk to you in there."

"What? I can't hear you."

No one moved. Alma's voice began to border on a shriek. "I said, come here!"

Ed set his beer can down on the table, which Alma had asked him not to do at least a thousand times, and he slouched slowly into the bedroom, where Alma sat in her easy chair, watching the small TV. She didn't look at him.

"You need to take the dog out."

"You called me all the way in here to tell me that? Why don't you take him?"

"I'm in the middle of something. I'm busy."

"Yeah, right. Busy watching some stupid program. It's your turn to take the stupid son of a bitch."

"I was in the middle of an interesting program and now I've probably lost the whole idea. OK, where's the damn leash?"

The stupid dog was listening and he watched all this with mournful eyes. He was stupid but he knew they were talking about him and he knew neither of them liked him. He whined to let them know that he really did need to go out.

Of course, this unpleasant struggle wasn't really about the dog.

And so went their marriage, like so many others, I'm afraid.

They'd been married slightly over two years when Ed had a head-on collision six miles out of town, coming home from a bar. He was the only fatality. Fault in the accident was never determined. Some said that was because of who Ed's daddy was. The car was totaled and Ed left Alma nothing except a small credit card debt and four cartons of empty beer cans stacked neatly in the back of the carport. And the dog.

Ed's funeral was a small sad affair. I guess most of them are, sad that is. It was reminiscent of the wedding, which some of the funeral attendees remembered because it hadn't been that long ago.

Ed's daddy came and he cried for a few minutes before he could compose himself. Ed's mama stayed at home. It was said that she was too grief stricken to be able to attend but a few unkind souls suggested that she might just be too drunk.

Alma returned the dog to the pound the next day.

Alma dropped her college course and the Tupperware gig and started working full-time at the dress shop. The college refused to give her a refund which was petty of them, but what can you do?

If Ed could've waited a few years, he might've inherited a bundle from his father, who dropped dead of a massive heart attack on the used car lot. Ed's daddy left nothing to Alma, not because he had anything against her, but because he just hadn't thought of it. He had no will and Ed's mother got everything, which was substantial.

The mother gave nothing to Alma and didn't include her in her own will. She thought Alma was beneath them and had trapped her boy into marriage with a fake pregnancy and she had a vague belief that Alma was somehow responsible for Ed's death, although Alma certainly had nothing to do with that.

Alma had a few moments of regret about this, about the money part that is, but she decided there wasn't anything she could do about it so she let it go and got on with her life, her life unencumbered by Ed or his family.

You may be wondering what happened to the poor dog. After it got to the shelter, was it adopted again or was it, as they say, "Put down?" You may wonder, but Alma didn't. She had a great ability to put things out of her mind when she wanted to, and honestly, as far as the dog, that didn't take much effort.

You also may be wondering how Alma felt about Ed's death. Well, there's no way to know, although we could make a reasonable guess. It's possible she had no feelings about it at all, whereas you and I, although certainly having no animosity towards Ed, might be stifling a cheer, especially if we could've known how things would unfold after that.

ALMA AS A WORKING GIRL

Before Ed's death, the staff at the dress shop were Alma, and the owner, and a string of part-time high school girls. By the time Alma started full-time, the owner had expanded the shop into the space next door and hired another full-time salesperson.

Alma devoted herself to the job and to developing herself as a salesperson. Home at night, she'd stand in front of the full-length mirror on her closet door and practice. She practiced different kinds of smiles and different snippets of patter. She wanted to come across to her customers as interested, even concerned, but not gushy or intrusive. She also experimented with different ensembles, hair do's, and make-up patterns. She wanted just the right balance, sophisticated but not threatening, and she found it. Her sales increased and the owner, realizing Alma was a good part of the reason the business was doing well, put her on commission in addition to her base salary. The owner also added a higher fashion line of clothing which attracted a more affluent clientele and carried a higher profit margin.

Alma developed a following, women who would request her advice and who'd ask her to call them when something they might like came in. She managed to make each woman feel as though they had a special secret relationship. They trusted Alma and her judgment, partly because she looked so good herself, partly because of the manner she'd so carefully developed, and partly because they thought she was honest with them, an appearance Alma also carefully cultivated.

"Dear, I don't think that dress gives you the look you want; it's not really you. And honestly, it's overpriced. I've been saving something in the back I think you'll like better, and it's less expensive."

Alma had never really known Ed's brother, Joey, two years the younger, and though smaller, a better athlete, baseball and track in high school and then playing baseball for the community college. This didn't totally explain why the father had so favored him over Ed, but it must've been part of it. Alma was surprised when Joey called late one evening.

"Hey, how you doing?"

"Who is this?"

"This is Joey. Don't you recognize me?"

He sounded like he might've been drinking.

"Joey who?"

"Cmon, Joey, Joey. Ed's brother."

"Oh."

Silence.

He spoke. "Well, how you doing?"

"Fine."

Silence, except she could hear him breathing. Then she was even more surprised,

"I thought we might get together."

"What?!"

"I said we might get together, you know, go out. What d'ya think?"

It took Alma a moment to catch her breath, but she didn't really need to do that to slam the receiver down. She never heard from Joey again. Two years later she read in the paper that Ed's mother had died. No details. Alma had no reaction at all.

Alma began making real money, most of which she carefully squirreled away in two different bank accounts and then in three. She didn't trust banks and she didn't want anyone, like the tellers, for example, to know too much of her business.

Alma lived frugally. She didn't particularly enjoy food and she never ate out, so food was a minimal expense. Alma had no interest in social activities, dating, or in the arts or politics. She of course never went to the movies. She had no TV.

She did go to a gym four times a week, where she worked out hard and without interaction with the other exercisees, though there were a few who nodded in recognition as they passed. Alma did her routine, checked her weight, showered and went home. Her appearance was one of her business assets, so she didn't mind that expense.

As her bank accounts grew, Alma became interested in the stock market, so she subscribed to a newspaper. Alma saw no sense in buying a book when she could read what she wanted for free from the library. She read a lot, business books and books about the stock market, although she recognized that the various authors often contradicted each other. She wondered why, if they knew so much about the market, they weren't just enjoying their riches instead of spending time writing books.

She'd never been good at math but she quickly grasped the concepts of upside potential versus downside risk, price-earnings ratios, and the beauty of compound interest.

Alma began dabbling in the market. She made some profit and lost more, but she was a quick learner and soon was keeping her losses small and her profits growing. She also was prudent, so when the market suffered a major setback and many people lost nearly everything, her losses were small and she made some bargain purchases at low prices.

The shop owner hired another full-time saleswoman and no longer used the high school girls. This pleased Alma because while she appreciated the girls' youth and liveliness, they didn't enhance the business. They weren't invested in it and weren't mature enough. Often customers would come in and wave the girls off to wait for Alma to serve them.

Alma was pleased with the two saleswomen, both a little older than her. They weren't friends but the three of them were cordial and learned from each other and weren't competing, partly because Alma was the only one on commission, a fact not known by the other two. The women seemed stable and likely to stick around and Alma liked that she wouldn't need to keep learning new personalities.

Alma became a super salesperson. She was especially good with the older wealthy ladies. By this time she was kind of wealthy herself. She was pleased with this, and surprised, but not much since this was a goal she'd set for herself early in life, to have a lot of money. Her stocks were doing well; she was taking fewer losses as she learned more about the market, and she could see her future unfolding on a good track.

Alma was good at the stock market, but she was also lucky. One afternoon she overheard two of her wealthy customers discussing a stock.

"It's a young company so there's lots of room for growth but it's been in business long enough to have a good reputation and looks like it's gonna stick around. And it has a niche, some kind of a specialty thing it makes and also the software to go with it, and technology is a good place to be nowadays."

"How do you know so much about it? Have you started doing research on stocks? I thought you let your broker handle your accounts?"

"He does, but my brother's girlfriend, this tall blonde, she's at least an inch taller than him, but they don't seem to mind, I mean she still wears heels when they go out. Anyway, she works there, at the company, she was saying they have so many orders they've had to hire a bunch of new people and she got a promotion, though I'm not sure why. I mean, she's nice enough, but she doesn't seem like the brightest bulb on the tree. So anyway, she was talking about this company and I asked my broker to check it out and he said it looked pretty good, he was going to buy some himself. So I just thought I'd let you know. You can ask your stock guy."

While Alma was showing dresses to the ladies, shepherding them in and out of the dressing rooms, making helpful comments and suggestions, she continued eavesdropping. That evening she went to the library and did her own research. She bought some stock in the company and when it went up a bit, instead of selling she bought some more. The company began a steady growth, spun off a part of itself into a new company, and both stocks continued to do well regardless of fluctuations in the market. That's the kind of stock anyone would like to own.

Seven years after Ed's death, Alma, like that company and like the dress shop, was doing well herself. I said she was kind of wealthy, but she wasn't ready to call herself rich yet. She wasn't where she wanted to be, but the future looked promising. Then she got another break, a big one.

But what else, you may be wondering, happened during those seven years? That's quite a chunk of time. Well, of course, things happened. There were elections. Wars. Catastrophes. But if you're wondering about what else happened with Alma, the answer would be, "Nothing much." The politics and current events never held much interest for her except as they affected the market; otherwise, they had no direct effect on her life.

So Alma worked and made more money. She read more financial books. She kept up her exercise and maintained her weight, which she seemed able to do without much effort, unlike some of us I could mention.

Did she have any love life; any dates?

No, she didn't. Sometimes a man would approach her but Alma had an air about her that discouraged this, and she easily rebuffed those who tried anyway.

"Well, what about her feelings?" you might ask. Yes indeed, what about Alma's feelings?

If during those seven years you'd asked Alma how she felt, she'd probably have said "I don't know," or, "OK."

If you'd pushed and asked her if she was happy, she might've said, "Happy, yes, of course," or she might've suggested you get lost.

Well, I guess she was kind of happy, but I think satisfied or comfortable might be a more accurate word.

You probably realize by now that Alma wasn't into feelings. Did she not have them, or had she learned how to not be aware of them? Take, for example, her brother's death. Remember her reaction, or its absence? Was it not a big deal because she had no attachment to him? Was she incapable of attachment, or had she learned to protect herself by not making attachments? So did she not have any grief? Or maybe she'd learned to not feel because she'd lacked the nurturing and support necessary to develop ways to cope with feelings.

Years later, after I again got interested in Alma, I discussed her lack of feelings and of self awareness with two professionals from our college student health center. They explained that if feelings are too uncomfortable, we can manage not to be aware of them, but they stay in our unconscious and can still cause problems. The psychiatrist also mentioned resilience, that some people manage to overcome the effects of a damaging childhood. I thought that must apply to Alma.

The psychiatrist had given me a look. "You seem to have become somewhat attached to her."

I thought about that for a moment. " I guess I have. Strange, because I never even met her."

He smiled. "Well, if it's any comfort, as a psychiatrist I've seen stranger things than that."

So, finally, back to the question of those seven years. OK, I guess one thing happened that affected her. The owner of her gym had a stroke and the gym closed. Alma had to find another gym, and learn a new routine because the equipment there was different, so there was a slight hassle. So if you insist that something more than I've revealed must've happened during seven years, I guess that was it; that was the biggest thing. In other words, as I said, nothing much.

But then—. But then—

ALMA'S BIG DISCOVERY

Alma was closing up the shop, seeing that all the dresses were hung just right for an appealing display, when she happened to glance at some papers on the owner's desk. Something caught her eye and she sat down in the owner's chair and read the papers. They were interesting. Alma discovered that the owner owned a number of shops under different aliases and they were not what they seemed. At least some of the shops were fronts for other businesses of questionable legitimacy. Some funny stuff was going on.

Alma carefully replaced the papers and finished closing up, in no rush but she was excited. The following day, on lunch break, she went to a lawyer. The next day, Alma asked the owner for a meeting.

They went into the office and the owner sat at her desk. She gestured at the chair in front of her desk. "Have a seat. What's up?"

Alma closed the office door behind her and remained standing, next to the chair.

She explained to the owner what she knew and suggested it was in the owner's best interest to get out of the businesses as quickly as possible before she got caught. The owner gasped. Alma offered to buy her out. When Alma mentioned the price she was offering, the owner gasped again. "That's ridiculous. This shop alone is worth more than that!"

Alma smiled and nodded. "Of course it is. But what's it worth to you to stay out of jail?"

"You're blackmailing me!"

Alma continued smiling. "I'm sorry you see it that way. I'm simply offering you a business proposition and a way to get out of this mess you're in. I'm trying to help you."

"You can go to hell!"

"You know, I could make this easier for you. I can take the books to an accountant and let him compare them with your tax returns. Then we can check and see if the DA is interested in the businesses. So you could see exactly where you stand. Would that help you make your decision?"

"Damn you! And after all I've done for you."

"I appreciate all you've done for me. I also know I've brought you a lot of business. But none of that's relevant now. We're talking about what an accountant and the IRS and maybe the district attorney might have to say."

The owner sputtered, "I'll have to think it over."

Alma said, "Fine. Think it over. Take all the time you need. But if you don't accept my offer, I'll need the afternoon off tomorrow to do what I need to do, as a law-abiding tax-paying citizen."

"That's a bunch of crap. I've given you a job and promoted you and helped you learn the business. This the way you treat me now? I ought to, ought to, I don't know what!"

The owner slammed her fist on the table and then she threw a paperweight across the room, but not at Alma. The paperweight was metal and so it didn't break, but it put a significant dent in the wall. Unfortunately, when she grabbed the paperweight, she knocked over her coffee mug which was on the desk next to it. The good news is that the mug was only half full, but still, the coffee spread over much of the desk and onto the papers there.

Alma pulled Kleenex out of her pocket and started mopping up the coffee, but she was careful not to get within arm's length of the owner.

"Noon tomorrow," Alma said. She got another Kleenex and started blotting the papers.

The owner glared at her. "You coldhearted bitch!"

Alma finished cleaning up and stood silently in front of the desk. Then she looked at her watch. The owner was mumbling to herself.

"Noon tomorrow," Alma repeated. "Unless you'd like to sign the papers now. I have them right here. My lawyer did them yesterday."

"Oh, shit," the owner exclaimed. "Shit. Give me the damn papers."

She glanced through them quickly and then slammed them down on the desk, which was reasonably dry now, although the bottom sheet would always carry a stain as a memento of the occasion. She angrily scrawled her signature.

Alma picked up the papers and looked at them. "There's another place, right here," she said, pointing. She put the middle paper back on the desk.

"Oh, shit," the owner moaned. But she signed.

"Thanks," Alma said. She gathered the papers and put them in her purse. "Please get your stuff and be out by closing. Oh, and please leave your keys on the desk."

"Go screw yourself!" were the owner's last words, ever, to Alma, who was closing the door behind her as she left, but she heard the parting shot. Alma smiled to herself and lightly clapped her hands.

There were empty boxes in the storeroom from a shipment of purses. The owner packed and carried her things to her car. It took her two trips. She said nothing to anyone. One of the salesladies thought this looked strange and she noticed the angry expression on the owner's face, but she was busy with a customer and thought no more about it until that evening.

Alma asked the two salesladies to stay a few minutes after closing, and she informed them that she'd bought the store. The older lady gasped, and the other said, "My! Well. Congratulations." They asked no questions.

Alma told them there'd be some changes; first, they'd both get a five percent raise starting the next day. The ladies thanked her. Then they all shook hands, said good night, and the ladies left. Alma stayed behind to lock up. She was eager to get home. Tomorrow would be a long day; she had a lot to do in the office, and she'd need to start recruiting at least one more salesperson and for the time being she'd still need to keep serving her special customers.

The ex-owner went home, packed and moved out of town that same week. She didn't leave the keys on the desk, but Alma had already arranged to have the locks changed. With what Alma paid her, the ex-owner wasn't wealthy, but she had enough to live comfortably, or not uncomfortably, at least for a while. She'd eventually need to pursue some other line of endeavor. She wasn't uncomfortable, but she wasn't happy.

That was of no consequence to Alma, who was busy untangling the various businesses from their shadier components. In some cases this wasn't easy because the people involved didn't want to be untangled. But Alma used her sales skills and intelligence and some of her cash and before long she was the twenty-seven-year-old owner of four dress shops, plus a men's clothing store which she promptly sold. She was a good salesperson and a tough bargainer and she made enough money from that sale to cover all the expenses of these transactions.

Alma replaced the managers of two of the shops with the two ladies she'd been working with. The older lady was reluctant to move out of state so far from her family but Alma made her an offer she couldn't refuse. The other out of state shop had been doing well and Alma kept that manager on and gave her a raise as well.

Alma didn't mind being busy. She was managing the original dress shop and overseeing her managers to make sure they were doing a good job and weren't swindling her. She paid them enough that they shouldn't be tempted and besides, they knew she was watching them. Closely. As one of them said to another on the phone, "She's nobody's fool."

Three of the shops thrived. After six months the shop managed by the younger salesperson was simply doing OK, and OK wasn't good enough for Alma. Alma was a good judge of people but not perfect, and the lady had been promoted to a position over her head. When Alma replaced her the relationship ended amicably enough. Alma preferred not to make enemies if she could avoid it; they might be able to do her some harm.

The now ex-manager called the older lady.

"Hi. This is Sue. Did you hear I got fired?"

"No! What!?"

"Yeah. Yesterday. Alma let me go."

"That's terrible. Why?"

"Well, Alma said the store wasn't meeting her expectations."

"That's cruel. You were in a tough location. And you hadn't really had time to get going. Alma's a cold fish. You must be really pissed."

"No, I was at first, but she gave me a good deal. So I'm happy. I'll take some time off, look around, find something good."

The older lady was thinking, "I hate to say it; Sue's good people, but she never was the sharpest knife in the drawer."

She said, "Well, I hope I'm going to be OK, after I moved here and all. Alma's never had a complaint.

"Mmmm," Sue paused. "She never complained to me either, maybe some hints. But a couple of times she said how well your store was doing. I think you'll be OK.

The older lady tried to soften things. "Maybe she had somebody else she wanted to put in there, a sister or something. Did you ever hear her say anything about family?"

"Not a word. She never said much of anything except business."

"Yeah. She kept to herself, buttered up those old ladies, sold those pricy dresses. I'm not saying she was snooty, but you couldn't call her friendly either. Anyway, guess I'm OK and you'll be alright. Alma knows what she's doing and what she wants, that's for sure. I mean, she started off as a salesgirl, just like us, and look at her now. Alma's nobody's fool."

"That's right, nobody's fool."

And they both did do OK. Sue got a good job, not as a manager. She realized managing wasn't really her thing. And the older lady kept making a good profit and getting bonuses. The original store kept growing, in size and profits. Alma added a separate department for an even more expensive line of clothes, where she specialized in attending to the wealthiest customers. She had a loyal clientele of rich women who were susceptible to being subtly flattered and made to feel special, and Alma had become an artist at this.

She managed to serve the rich ladies and keep her eye on everything else at the same time. Soon the store was drawing more customers, rich ones, from further distances. Alma spent little on advertising, but word of mouth was powerful. "You look gorgeous in that, Honey! It's unique. Where in the world did you get it?"

For two years Alma was busy handling business but comfortable. Once again, nothing much happened in her life during those years.

A big chain offered to buy the stores. Alma turned them down but said she might consider a higher offer, much higher. She also said she wouldn't deal with the same junior executive; she thought he must be the inept relative of some higher up.

She'd researched the company and identified a vice president. "And don't send that kid again. If you're serious, have Howard Thurston give me a call."

Alma and Howard had several meetings, and he took her to dinner, which became almost intimate, but still, Alma was tough. "Look, the shops are all growing and I see a big future. And I enjoy running them (a slight exaggeration). I don't need to sell and what would I do with myself if I did? So don't insult me with these low ball offers."

Howard finally offered something close to the "much higher" that Alma had in mind, and the deal was signed. They parted pleasantly but Howard caught some flak back at the office for being out negotiated by a woman.

One day Alma was the fairly well off owner of four dress shops and the next, she was a retiree with three point eight million from the sale of the stores and a stock portfolio of one point one million, which she quickly liquidated as she no longer had any reason to take a risk. In fact, the market had another large setback two months after she liquidated.

Alma had been so busy managing the shops and then negotiating the sale and then reallocating her funds that she hadn't given much thought to what she'd do next. She bought a house in a good neighborhood, a nice house but not ostentatious nor extravagant. Then she booked a long cruise during which she intended to plan the rest of her life. Which didn't look bad. Really, not bad at all.

ALMA'S FIRST CRUISE

Alma enjoyed her cruise. It was quiet and restful and gave her time to think. The other passengers soon realized she didn't welcome their friendly advances and they left her alone. She did form a relationship of sorts with her cabin steward, who was extra attentive to her. After all, she was obviously richer than most of the other passengers, wasn't unkind to him, and wasn't bad looking, really not bad looking at all, although this wasn't very important as the steward was gay, which Alma suspected, but didn't matter to her.

The steward spent extra time cleaning Alma's cabin and before long he began telling Alma about his life as a steward and about growing up in the Philippines, without bringing up the gayness, and what he knew about some of the other passengers. Alma found his conversation mildly interesting and out of habit she listened for any information that might help in making profitable investments. They both enjoyed their interactions, he more than she, because she seemed an attentive and sympathetic listener. The tip she gave him at the end of the cruise was about what he'd been hoping for when he forced himself to be realistic.

Everyone on the cruise except a few chronic complainers said the food was quite good but Alma didn't care as long as it wasn't bad. She didn't take any of the ship's side trips, but stayed in her cabin or out on the deck when the weather was good, which was most of the time. She read a lot, again business, finance, the market, but that was just to pass the time; she wasn't really interested in that anymore but those were the books she'd brought with her. The ship's library was good, yet had little of interest for Alma. She spent a lot of time just looking at the ocean and thinking. She was thirty-two, rich, healthy, intelligent, and not bad looking. She should have a good life ahead.

Alma was thinking about her options. I can't say she was *considering* her options because nothing she could think of was attractive enough to actually consider. "Considering" would imply there might be a chance she would do it after weighing the pros and cons. No, she was just thinking of options and rejecting them. Volunteering? Not her style. And volunteering to do what? She couldn't think of anything that might interest her. Buying another store? Yuck. Been there, done that. Get a job? She couldn't imagine working for somebody else again. She liked making money and it was satisfying to do well in the stock market, but now, with plenty of money, that didn't seem appealing, even as a hobby. She wasn't about to start going to casinos or racetracks and socializing wasn't her game and who would she socialize with? Certainly not the wealthy women who'd been her customers, most of whom she considered shallow and stupid, and a social relationship with their former shop girl wouldn't be appropriate or comfortable for anyone.

Alma went through a long list of possibilities: politics, sports, games, designing, consulting, writing and on and on—nope, nope, nope and nope again.

When she got off the ship, Alma felt relaxed but also frustrated about still being at loose ends. She did some decorating of her house, but it was in good shape when she bought it and she was pretty satisfied with it as it was. She continued going to the gym four times a week and she started taking long walks, partly for her health and to keep her looks up and partly from boredom. But things have a way of happening and the state of boredom didn't last long.

ALMA DISCOVERS LITERATURE AND ANTHONY DISCOVERS HER

On a walk, Alma went into a coffee shop in a nearby mall, although this wasn't like her; she liked to keep going and she liked being by herself. But it was a warm day and she was thirsty. She sat down and ordered a medium iced coffee and a large glass of water. She looked around and decided she liked the shop. It wasn't a fast food kind of place but it wasn't frilly or pretentious either, just a nice clean coffee shop with comfortable chairs and not loud or crowded. And the coffee was good. So on another walk, she went back again. And then again.

Soon Alma noticed the manager, a young woman, a girl really. Alma identified her as "a go-getter" which she liked, especially in a woman. But Alma had been going there for nearly a year before they exchanged any significant words. A new waiter clumsily spilled coffee on Alma's skirt. The manager, alert to what was happening, rushed over and began trying to make things right.

"I'm so sorry."

"Well, it's not a big deal, and he didn't do it on purpose, but the skirt was clean."

"I am sorry. He's new. We'll comp you the coffee."

"Well, I certainly think so; I wasn't about to pay for it." Alma chuckled.

"Of course not. I meant you'll get another cup, no charge. And how about a nice pastry or something? Is there anything else I could get you?"

Alma had, in fact, noticed some scones that looked attractive, but she wasn't that interested in food, and she replied, "No, thank you."

"OK, well, let me know. If the skirt has to be dry cleaned, just bring in the bill next time and we'll make it right."

"No, I can just wash it. It won't be a problem. Just have someone else bring me a new iced coffee and we'll let it go."

"Surely. I'll bring it myself. And thank you for being so understanding."

"Just bring my coffee please."

The manager said OK and soon more coffee appeared. The manager was so alert she'd even noticed Alma glancing at the scones and she also brought one on a saucer. But Alma didn't touch it.

With the ice broken, Alma and the manager occasionally had brief chats. Alma learned the manager was working her way through college. This impressed Alma, but she wasn't impressed that she was majoring in American studies, whatever the hell that is. She wondered what kind of future that might lead to. Strangely enough, they still didn't know each other's names.

As the future turned out, even after she graduated the girl continued to manage the coffee shop so the education seemed to have had no practical benefit. But both Alma and the manager were lovers of education, of expanding themselves, of learning for the sake of learning. But we're getting ahead of our story.

This relationship, if you could call it that, continued for a while before Alma learned the manager's name, which eventually became a necessity because of a business matter. But I can tell you now that her name was Arnid.

To be clear, Alma never regarded Arnid as like a daughter, although there was a tendency to regard her as like a younger sister. And at this point, she actually had a closer relationship, little though it was, with Arnid than with her sisters.

Alma had been going to the shop almost a year and chatting with the manager less than that when she abruptly bought the place. Only then did she learn Arnid's name.

She'd been enjoying her coffee and the quiet of the shop when she was annoyed by a busboy noisily clearing tables and dropping the silverware into his tray. "Clang! Clang!" It was the same lad who'd spilled coffee on her; he'd been demoted to busboy because of his clumsiness. Next, Alma noticed that her waitress, who was new, had overcharged her. She called the waitress over.

"Excuse me, but you've overcharged me here," showing her the check.

"Huh?"

"You've charged me for two coffees and I only had one."

"No, you had two."

"No, I had one. One coffee. That's what I always have. One."

"I think you had two."

"No." Alma's mouth tightened. She didn't want to be rude or crude, but she was getting more annoyed.

Arnid, who did keep her eye on the place, came to the table. "Is there a problem?"

"No," Alma said. "No problem. How are you doing?"

"I'm fine, thank you. I just graduated, finally. Are you sure everything is OK?"

"Yes, indeed. Congratulations. What are you planning to do now?"

"I think I'll stay here. I like it. I may take another course or two, but I like this job."

"Well, good then," Alma said. "Who owns this place?"

"Are you going to make a complaint?"

"Oh, no, not at all. But who is the owner? And can you get me the phone number?"

Arnid said, "Wait just a minute," and walked into the office.

She returned with the name and phone number on a yellow sticky. "I hope there's not a problem," she said as she handed it to Alma.

"None at all," said Alma, "Thank you very much." She folded the yellow sticky and put it in her pants pocket. "Be seeing you."

Alma walked out without paying, leaving the check on the table. Arnid tore it in half and threw it in the wastebasket.

When she got home, Alma called the shop owner. He personally answered quickly. She introduced herself and said, "I'd like to buy the coffee shop."

Not surprisingly he was surprised. "It's not for sale."

"How much do you want for it?"

"It's not for sale."

"How about—?" and Alma mentioned a figure.

"No, that's not enough."

"OK, how about—?" Alma mentioned a figure significantly higher.

"Are you serious?"

"Absolutely."

"How were you planning to pay for it?"

"Cash."

"Cash?" the man gasped.

"Yes, cash. I'll have my lawyer call you and do the paperwork and bring you the check."

"OK," the man said, "OK. Make it a certified check, though." He'd wondered if this was a joke or a scam, but Alma had made him an offer he couldn't refuse and somehow she'd been convincing. He was a little stunned.

Alma didn't actually have a lawyer but her accountant found one. Alma was pleased that the lawyer was a woman and that she handled everything. She brought the papers to the house and Alma gave her a check and soon Alma owned the coffee shop.

Alma still didn't know the name of the manager, who, she assumed, didn't know hers. That was a false assumption though, because the manager had seen her credit card and the owner, the ex-owner, had called Arnid and told her about the sale. So the next time Alma entered the shop, Arnid came up to her and said, "Well, congratulations! And welcome."

Alma smiled. "I guess at this point we should know names. I'm Alma."

"Arnid."

They shook hands and Alma beckoned Arnid to sit. They discussed the shop.

Alma knew she'd paid too much for the shop, but she didn't care. All of this was decidedly unAlmaish, to drop into a coffee shop, to do anything impulsively, or to pay too much for anything. But that's what she did.

The next day, Wednesday, Alma met with Arnid and Jose, the chef. Alma asked about any improvements they'd like. The chef mentioned a top of the line oven stove combination, knowing it was too expensive, but he thought if he asked for too much, he might get something pretty good. He was stunned when Alma just said, "Fine." Arnid said she'd love to have an addition on the back of the building for a larger office. Then the staff could use her present office for a lounge and changing room. Alma said, "Sure, great idea." Arnid agreed to bring in some paint and cloth samples so they could choose a new décor. They decided to keep the same name.

Friday morning, Alma personally fired the clumsy busboy and the rude waitress, not for the satisfaction but because she felt it wouldn't be fair to burden Arnid with that, since it was her own decision. The two were not happy getting fired but they perked up when Alma said they'd each get two thousand dollars severance pay. They'd never heard of anyone in the food service business getting severance pay, and certainly not them.

Alma had called Arnid the day before to tell her that the two would be going so Arnid had already found replacements. She had no trouble finding good ones after Alma told her everyone would get a ten percent raise. In addition, Alma was offering a health insurance plan and a small retirement plan, which startled the staff.

The shop closed for three weeks for the remodeling; Alma'd offered a bonus to the contractor if it was finished on time and it was. The staff were paid full salary for the three weeks. When Alma and Arnid and Jose were satisfied with the remodeling, Jose more than satisfied, the shop reopened. Alma wasn't interested in running anything anymore, and she trusted Arnid to run the shop as she pleased. It was nice to drop in and know the place belonged to her. The staff treated her with only a little extra deference, which suited Alma fine. Still, eventually, there was a problem.

The shop was more attractive, the food and service better, the prices unchanged, and the shop got busier. Arnid was pleased but Alma wasn't. They agreed on a plan. They'd continue the European tradition, customers could occupy a table and dawdle over their coffee or whatever as long as they wished, but laptops were banned. They got an electronic sign to display the wait time for a table, and if over ten minutes the sign said "Full." Alma's favorite table was reserved for her, which further cut down customers. This wasn't going to be another place ruined by success, not if Alma could help it.

Arnid worried that these changes would hurt their profits. Alma told Arnid not to worry, she wasn't measuring success by the profit. She did compromise and they raised the prices slightly. This satisfied Arnid although she couldn't help keeping an eye on the numbers. The profit was indeed less than preAlma but it was steady and Arnid was comfortable once she saw Alma meant what she'd said. They had a nice coffee shop where people could relax in comfort and quiet, and it was providing a decent living and a comfortable work environment for the staff of eleven, who functioned well together and enjoyed working there.

Alma was sitting in the coffee shop, her coffee shop, her table, turning the pages of a financial magazine she wasn't interested in. She picked up a paperback novel someone had left on a nearby table. It was by an author named Puryear. She'd never heard of him; few people had. It was partly about a guy riding the ups and downs of trading in the stock market, and she began reading it. She was surprised that she got interested in what was going to happen to him because she usually didn't have much interest in other people, except to know them as customers so she could do a good selling job. Well, the ship steward had been kind of interesting and she did like Arnid and now she was interested in what was going to happen to some character in a novel. Alma finished that book and went to the library and checked out six more novels. She realized that fiction was interesting to her, although she only liked three of those novels. As she began reading novels regularly a new world opened for her.

This led to an increase in the length and frequency of her chats with Arnid, who had studied American literature. They often read the same novels, and their different viewpoints and strong opinions fostered interesting discussions. Arnid believed one needed to read classics, ranging from *Moby Dick* to *The Catcher in the Rye* and *Catch 22*, to better appreciate newer works. She recommended these to Alma and Alma liked most of them.

Alma sat at her table with a glass of iced coffee, reading a complicated novel about a complicated family. She felt someone looking at her. She glanced up and saw a nice-looking man peering in her direction but trying to do it discreetly. Of course, it's difficult to peer discreetly. She turned back to her book. In a moment he was standing at her table, possibly emboldened by her glance. He asked what she was reading. She showed him the cover. He wasn't satisfied, "No, I mean what's it about?"

Alma briefly explained, "It's about a complicated mixed-up family. Kind of a mess really."

"Well, I probably don't need to read that; I've lived it. I'm Anthony, by the way."

He was even better looking up close.

"Alma."

"My real name's Tony, but in high school there were so many Tonys and Anthony sounded more genteel, so I changed it."

"Funny, me, too. I'm actually Mary Alma, but I started going by Alma in high school because Mary was so common."

"Interesting. I grew up in an Italian neighborhood; there were lots of us Tony's. It's funny, most of them were really Anthonys."

"Yeah, our school was mostly Catholic and there was a flood of Marys. "

Anthony laughed. "Sorry. That's a funny image, a flood of Marys. So you grew up Catholic, too?"

"Sort of. We weren't that involved in it. Oh, I guess my mother was. She went to church when she could."

"My family was Catholic, capital C, mass every morning before work, fish on Fridays, the whole works."

"You had a big family?" Alma asked.

"Oh, Lord, yes. Five boys and two girls. You could call it big, alright."

By this time, Anthony was seated at the table although Alma hadn't invited him. She thought, "Hey, what's he doing? I need to careful." She was surprised that she didn't object.

Anthony was quite good looking.

He'd acknowledged his big family and he asked, "You?"

"We were just four kids, at first anyway. We shrunk.

"Oh? What happened?"

Alma told him about her brother dying, and about her sister getting kicked out. She didn't mention the drinking or the abuse, but still, this was amazingly quick intimacy, especially for Alma, but Anthony had an engaging manner, asked intelligent sensitive questions, and was a good listener.

Anthony smiled. "So your family was complicated, like mine and like the book."

"Oh, I don't know. I don't think so. Really, pretty normal, pretty average."

Did Alma somehow manage to actually believe this, or was it just her typical reaction of being wary and closed off? Who knows?

"OK," Anthony replied, possibly being sensitive enough to recognize a brick wall or a sore spot when he ran into it. "What else you been reading?" They talked some more about books and then Anthony said he had to go. He asked if they could meet again at the coffee shop and Alma said yes.

They met again in a few days. This time Anthony sat down at once. Alma was reading another Puryear book and Anthony again started the conversation by asking about the book. Alma explained why she liked this author and Anthony said he didn't care for him. He thought the author was trying to imitate Hemingway with his sparse style and wasn't doing a good job of it. But then sometimes Puryear seemed to be trying to be Saramago, with his run on sentences. Anthony thought they were annoying, sloppy, and showed a lack of discipline. He didn't care for this author. And he thought there was too much emphasis on money.

Alma knew who Hemingway was, though she'd never read anything of his and had no idea of his style. She'd only recently started reading fiction, which she'd considered a frivolous waste of time and had avoided since high school, when she'd been required to read *Silas Marner* and *The Scarlet Letter,* which she thought were duller than dirt. She'd never heard of Saramago, but she wasn't about to reveal her lack of knowledge to this stranger.

Anthony continued, "Hemingway and Saramago! Come on. He should develop his own style."

Alma's mouth tightened. "Maybe that is his own style?"

Anthony's response was brief, "Hmpfhh."

Alma thought for a moment. She said, "Well, he's not my favorite author," not mentioning how few fiction authors she'd read. "But I like his books. His sparse style and not much description lets us use our imagination, so we get more of an emotional response. Like our image of the villain comes from our idea of what a villain would look like instead of from his, for example. And maybe the run-on sentences show a sense of urgency or how tightly connected events or ideas are. And the emphasis on money seems pretty realistic these days."

Alma didn't need to defend Puryear nor her taste, she was just explaining her viewpoint, and she was also clarifying it for herself.

Did you notice when Alma mentioned "an emotional response?" Weren't you a little surprised? I was. Sounds very unAlmaish.

Anthony listened to her attentively and said, "I see your point. It just doesn't work that way for me." He repeated his dislike of the emphasis on money, and this led to a discussion of what money had been like in their families which led to a discussion of their experiences around alcohol. This degree of sharing and openness so soon seems amazing if you know anything about Alma.

Alma had learned in her childhood to be suspicious, always on guard. She'd wondered at once if Anthony was after her money. She didn't know what he did for a living or if he did anything. Maybe he lived off of picking up rich women. So on their second meeting, she certainly wouldn't call it a date, she asked him what he did.

"Work, you mean?" he asked.

"Yes, of course."

"Well, I do lots of other things besides work, thank God, but I'm an architect."

Alma learned that Anthony owned a small architectural firm, had degrees in architecture and English literature, had meant the "Thank God" sincerely, being religious, and wasn't after her money.

Their sharing led to more intimacy, and they had some actual dates, not just coffee shop meetings, and one thing led to another, as they will, and then to another, and then - .

I could tell you more about this, but it went about as you'd expect, just more slowly because of Alma's wariness, and frankly, it's not that interesting. If you'd been hoping for some bodice ripping hot romantic stuff or some Hollywood on again off again and running towards each other in the rain stuff, you'd be disappointed.

Just to reaffirm that Anthony wasn't after her money, when he finally moved in with Alma, he insisted on paying rent, even though she owned the house free and clear and she didn't want or need any money from him.

With Anthony, Alma expanded her life. She read more novels, and a wider range of nonfiction, and they discussed what she was reading. She liked Jane Austin and some of Faulkner, but not *The Great Gatsby*.

"What didn't you like about it?"

"I don't really know. I just didn't."

"Did you learn something about those times and that culture?"

"Yeah. I guess that was worth something, the flappers, and the rich and the superficiality. But I didn't like Gatsby himself. That probably made me not like the book."

"Do you have to like the protagonist to like a book?"
"Maybe that's it."
"How about Lolita? Did you like that book?"
"Oh, that Hummer or whatever. That guy?"
"Yep, Humbert."
"Ugh! He wasn't appealing, was he? But I guess I enjoyed the book, kind of."
"What if a book was interesting or informative, but not really enjoyable, per se? Would you say you liked it?"

Anthony was more knowledgeable than Alma, but he was impressed at how quickly she caught onto things and he never looked down on her in spite of her lack of education. Alma began to enjoy music, not classical, but other genres from Anthony's CDs and from visiting jazz and blues clubs. Neither Alma nor Anthony were much of a drinker; in fact, Alma had never tasted anything except beer, and that only twice, with Ed, but she developed an appreciation of fine wines, which she could easily afford.

One thing that didn't develop, despite Anthony's efforts, was an expanded social life. Alma wouldn't engage with his friends or business associates and Anthony went out without her, which was fine with Alma; she was comfortable being alone. And she adamantly resisted his attempts to expose her to anything religious, like a church service or visiting an empty church to enjoy the art or the architecture. And she wouldn't discuss anything religious or spiritual. So Anthony occasionally attended mass alone, which was also OK with Alma.

"What's your thing about church, anyway?" Anthony was genuinely curious.
"I don't like it. It's boring. Actually, I think it's all nonsense."
"You don't believe in God?"
"I either don't believe in him or I don't like him."
"What if God is a Her and not a Him. Does God have genitals? Or x and y chromosomes?"

"I don't know. I don't want to talk about it."

"Why not? Am I making you uncomfortable?"

Alma's mouth tightened. "No. I just don't want to talk about it I told you."

Anthony dropped it. He wasn't trying to convert her, just to have a discussion, but clearly that wasn't possible.

Alma rarely thought about God but when she did, her thoughts were not positive. She thought God should've made the world better than it was, without so much suffering. "If this was the best he could do, who needs him?" She didn't connect her resentment to her childhood because she also rarely thought about her childhood.

Alma feared God, not the fear taught in catechism class, but people with ungratified dependency longings, even unconscious, sometimes cope by becoming hyper independent, and the idea of a God you could depend on was threatening. Of course, she would've strongly, perhaps angrily, denied these longings if you'd suggested them.

Alma had never experienced someone liking her for herself and not for what she could do for them. Actually, her father had, but any positive memories of him were overridden by the negative ones and she would've laughed, bitterly, if you'd suggested any of this to her. So this new experience of being appreciated by Anthony had a powerful pull on her.

Alma and Anthony relished their relationship. They were fond of each other, but neither of them ever said the L word, Alma because she was too wary and because she didn't know how to say it. Love had never been a significant factor in her life. She had never used the word and had heard it applied to her only twice, when Ed was trying to maneuver her into the back seat of his Chevy. And Anthony had his own reasons for not using it, whatever they were.

Alma enjoyed the sense of expanding, enjoying things she'd never even thought about before. She liked learning. She appreciated that Anthony was helping her grow as a person.

And Alma thought Anthony was good in bed. She'd had orgasms before, but never this good or this consistently. Of course, aside from the occasional guilty solitary sin, she only had Ed to compare him to and Ed's style had been `Wham! Bam! Thank you, Ma'am,' absent the `Thank you, Ma'am' part.

Alma and Anthony had been together a year when she got the call about her father. She'd kept occasional phone contact with her mother but she never visited although her mother always mentioned that a daughter owed at least a call a week and certainly visits on holidays. Alma didn't agree and her mother's complaining, criticizing, and guilt provoking didn't incite a strong urge for more contact.

The call came from one of her mother's church friends. She said the mother was too distraught to talk. Her father had bled to death in his car in the garage, coughing up blood from ruptured esophageal varicose veins. A half empty bottle of vodka was on the floorboard.

Her mother was overwhelmed so Alma handled all the funeral arrangements. She kept them modest and footed the bill without asking her mother about it. Being busy with arrangements and finances helped her avoid feeling anything about her father's death if she'd needed any help to do that.

Her mother told everyone the cause of death was a heart attack but when Alma read the death certificate it said cirrhosis of the liver. The service was in the funeral home, not the church, since her father hadn't been Catholic, but her mother had managed to get a priest to do the service, which Alma walked out in the middle of because she couldn't stand the bullshit.

Her mother asked Alma to clean the car, which Alma declined, so the task fell to her mother's friend. She must've been quite a friend, or perhaps she was something of a martyr. Anyway, Alma's father got buried and the car got cleaned.

And that was that.

LIFE GOES ON FOR ALMA, BUT NOT EXACTLY

After her father's death, life went on, pleasantly, for two and a half more years, give or take a couple of months.

Alma went to an opera just to please Anthony although she expected to hate it. Fortunately, the opera was Mozart's Cosa Fan Tutti, and she enjoyed it immensely. After seven operas, they realized she liked light operas and didn't care at all for heavy ones, so it was fortunate that her first opera was Mozart or she would've lost out on enjoying opera at all. She especially didn't care for the Wagner opera she tried to sit through but left after the interminable first act. She persuaded Anthony to stay because he was enjoying it and she took a cab home. She settled down with the novel she was in the middle of. She was intrigued by the story and had to find out what happened to the characters. She'd been asleep for well over an hour before Anthony finally got home.

They went to a few art galleries. Anthony loved them, especially because he was an architect, but not Alma. "Why waste time looking at pictures when there's was so much real stuff to see if you want to see something?"

Anthony said maybe she just wasn't a visual person, "Was there anything there you liked?"

"Well, maybe Van Gogh. I didn't like his pictures, but the way he used colors was kind of nice. Like that bedroom picture, with the bed. That caught my eye. But the picture was ugly. And the self portrait. Why look at that? I might've liked to see a photo of him instead. Anyway, I wanted to ask you, what is art? I mean, some of the things in there were just things. Why were they art?"

"Good question. Maybe art's anything that's produced to be looked at?"

Alma patted the chair she was sitting on. "So if I set this wine glass on this chair, and then said, `Hey, Anthony, look at this,' I could call it art?"

"Maybe. I guess so. Especially if you set it a particular way, like in the center, or on the edge, deliberately, so that it looked a certain way, that could be art."

"That makes no sense to me. Would that take any talent? Couldn't any three-year-old do that? I mean, some of that stuff in the museum could've been done by a three-year-old."

"Interesting point. There's some paintings by young kids, or even a gorilla, and I think an elephant, that've actually sold as art."

"Um. Ok, I think it's just not my thing. And by the way, look at this. Did you notice this glass is empty?" She held it up and waved it. "Another half glass of the white, please? Just a half."

Anthony was good about accepting Alma's tastes. He didn't try to change her mind or push her to do anything she really didn't want to do, although he encouraged her to a least try something before deciding she didn't like it.

So Anthony helped Alma explore new experiences, but they spent most evenings pleasantly at home reading and discussing books. They were both bright and Anthony had a degree in English, so their discussions had depth and were engaging.

Anthony made one more attempt at the religious thing.

"I just read a great book by Anne Lamott, you might enjoy it."

"What's it about?"

"Well, it's slightly religious, but very different. She's kind of off the grid. It's funny."

"Religious! Nope, no, none, never. Got it?" Alma's tone bordered on harsh.

"OK, OK. Sorry. Still, I really wish you'd read *For the Time Being,* Annie Dillard. It's my favorite book maybe, and I'd love to discuss it with you. It's so much more than religious, and she's got this wonderful unique style."

"You keep trying, don't you? I know religion's important to you, so I don't knock it, I just don't want it. That's you, this is me, and that's it. Haven't you read anything else interesting lately? Something I might like?"

Neither Alma nor Anthony could've said exactly when things started to unravel, nor why. But moments of tension started to creep in, and then minutes of tension, and then - well, you can see where this is going.

Alma appreciated her changes, her growth, but she felt Anthony was pushing her too fast, too far beyond her comfort zone, and expecting too much of her. She was enjoying her new life and new experiences, but she remembered that she hadn't been unhappy before them.

Anthony was enjoying her company, and her bed, and watching her grow. He saw himself as the architect of this growth. Each time Alma tried something new and liked it, it made him feel good about Alma and about himself. But while Alma was progressing a little too fast for her comfort, she was progressing a little too slowly for Anthony's satisfaction, and that's where the tension began.

"You know, tomorrow there's a good concert in the cathedral, and the architecture there's worth a trip itself. I'd really like to show you some of the details, stuff most people wouldn't notice or understand. It's nothing at all about religion; it's about music and architecture. I'd really like you to come."

"Why would you even ask me that? You know I won't go to the cathedral no matter what was there. I wouldn't go for the second coming of Jesus Christ with all his angels. So why would you ask me? Why?"

"Well, I can always hope, can't I. I mean, you've liked things you didn't know about before, but I swear, sometimes you can be close-minded. I mean you decided before you even considered it."

"That's right; I decided years ago. No, no cathedral. You should know me by now. So there's no reason for you to ask me things like that. It's obnoxious."

Anthony only said, "Hmph," and picked up his book. Alma picked up hers. There was no literary discussion that night or indeed any more conversation at all, unless you count the perfunctory "Good nights."

Alma couldn't have explained her aversion to religion if Anthony had asked, but he now knew better than to do that.

Alma had learned early that life was dangerous and uncertain; at any moment the ground could suddenly open beneath you and whoosh! - you'd be swallowed up. You needed to be wary, aware of everything and prepared for anything. Ed's unexpected death had reinforced this insecurity, even though she hadn't been attached to him.

But if she could be alert enough, know enough, control enough, maybe she could prevent the catastrophe. Controlling small things, the things she could control, helped her maintain the illusion that she could control it all. This helped suppress the fear, the terror actually, that still lurked in the basement of her mind.

So the tension with Anthony increased Alma's insecurity which led to behavior that annoyed Anthony. Alma began having complaints for the first time.

"Anthony, you left your shoes out again. How many times do I have to tell you?"

"OK. Sorry. I just forgot."

"You're always forgetting. Maybe you just don't care."

"OK. They're in the closet now. What's the big deal? Let's drop it, OK?"

"It's frustrating. It's a mess in here. And somebody could trip over them. I'm asking you and asking you and it's like you don't even listen. You're not a kid anymore, you know."

With a "Hmph," Anthony left the room.

Two evenings later, Alma prepared a light dinner, green salad topped with fresh anchovies, French bread and a chilled bottle of an excellent chardonnay. Anthony was enjoying it.

"Alma, this is very good. Pass the butter, will you?"

"Couldn't you say please? I'm not your waitress you know."

"Yes, of course I know. So now would you please just pass the damn butter please?"

Another time, he'd done her the favor of returning her books to the library and he'd missed one:

She held the book up. "You left this book on the table."

"Oh, sorry. I didn't see it."

"You didn't see it. I guess you didn't really look. It was right there."

"I said I was sorry."

Alma's mouth tightened. "Sorry? OK, but now I have to make an extra trip to the library."

We know Alma was going to the library frequently anyway, and so a trip wouldn't be extra, or even if it was extra, so what? But that wasn't really the point, was it?

Anthony backed away some. He didn't offer to massage her neck as often and he spent more evenings with his friends. He still asked her to come with him, knowing she'd refuse and beginning to be glad of that.

Alma had allowed Anthony, and also their life together, to become important to her and she grew increasingly fearful of losing them. More insecure, she became more vigilant and controlling, so Anthony became more annoyed and distant, which made Alma feel more insecure, which -. It unfolded, slowly at first and then faster and faster, snowballing.

Anthony, of course, hadn't had a perfect childhood, so he brought his own stuff to the party; it wasn't all Alma. Maybe he wasn't as self-confident and secure as he seemed and was a little controlling himself. Maybe he had a need to see Alma grow under his nurturing and was pushing a little too much not solely from altruism and affection for Alma but to satisfy his own needs.

Maybe Anthony, like Alma, had difficulties around the L word. Maybe he had issues from being raised by a single mother and never knowing his father. But this story is about Alma, not Anthony, so we won't go into his stuff, tempting though that may be. That's a whole different story.

So the couple had their tensions, and then their grievances, and then their spats, which were never more than spats because they both kept some control over themselves. Then, finally, they had their discussion, or "The Discussion" as they referred to it.

They'd settled down for their after-dinner evening as usual, but Anthony didn't pick up a book.

"Alma, I've been thinking."

"Me, too. What've you been thinking?"

"Well, you know I really care about you. You do know that, don't you?"

"Yes, but-?"

"It's not the same now, is it?"

"No, that's for sure."

Silence.

"Alma, we've had a good time; I mean I have and I think you have too, right?"

"I believe you're speaking in the past tense."

"Alma, don't you think it's time now?

"Yes, yes I do. There's no point in going on this way. It's not doing either of us any good."

"OK, thank you for being so reasonable. I guess we're both feeling the same way. You're a nice person, nothing wrong with you. And you haven't done anything wrong."

"No, I certainly haven't. But you're not satisfied with me anymore, or with being with me. And I'm not satisfied with that. Don't you think a clean break would be best?"

"Probably so. This hurts, but I think if we draw it out, it'll just be worse."

Anthony was hoping Alma would say that it would be painful for her, too, and maybe she was thinking that. Or maybe not.

Alma's response was businesslike. "I agree. Let's get to the logistics."

The Discussion was surprisingly cool, in the sense of dispassionate, not in the sense of "neat." Both were surprised to find the other in immediate agreement that it was time, it wasn't working, separation was inevitable and best for both of them. And they agreed it would be silly to talk about staying "just friends" after how they'd been. They refrained from blaming or finger-pointing, although the temptation was there. They had no children or pets and they were living in Alma's house and had bought nothing together so there was nothing to squabble over.

They were civilized and mature and they tried to be kind. They still had affection for each other. If there were other feelings they managed to manage them.

Anthony wasn't prepared for how fast it went; he hadn't expected to leave that evening. He said he'd stay with a friend while he looked for a place. They agreed that his stuff, clothes, CD's and the few paintings he'd brought with him could stay until he found a place. Alma finally said he could stay in the spare bedroom until then, but he declined, as she'd hoped.

Anthony went into the bedroom, packed a suitcase, came back in ten minutes, gave Alma a hug, and let himself out. He didn't slam the door and Alma appreciated that. And it was over, that quickly. Two and a half years, give or take a few months. Over.

And that was that.

Alma had no idea that Hank was just around the corner, so to speak.

ALMA'S NEXT PHASE AND HANK

After the door clicked behind Anthony, Alma sat on the sofa for a few minutes. She wasn't stunned. She wasn't sad. She wasn't trying to figure it out, to understand it; that wasn't Alma. But she was already feeling at loose ends again, although she wasn't considering her options yet. She poured herself half a glass of wine, white, and pulled a book from the bookshelf. She read and sipped her wine for forty-five minutes. Then she turned out the lights and went to bed. She slept soundly and had no dreams that she could recall the next morning.

Six weeks later in the checkout line at her neighborhood market the man behind her tapped her arm. "Excuse me, Miss. I notice you've got a carton of shrimp there in your basket. Do you know where those shrimp came from?"

Alma said she didn't.

"Do you mind if I take a look at the package?"

She looked at him strangely but said, "OK."

He picked up the package and examined it carefully, then set it back in the basket.

"These look OK," he said. "I think they're alright." And he nodded a few times.

"What?" was her response.

Hank explained that there'd been a recent outbreak of salmonella from shrimp imported from Thailand and one of his neighbors had been very sick and he didn't want that to happen to her. But these shrimp weren't from Thailand, they were from the Gulf. They should be safe if she kept them properly refrigerated.

"Oh. Well, thanks. Thanks for looking out for me." She pushed her basket forward.

"It's sure a long line," he observed. "They're usually not this busy on a weekday."

Alma nodded.

"Yeah, it's sure a long line," he said again.

Alma turned to half face him.

She guessed he was a couple of years younger than her. He was dressed casually but looked clean. She noted that he was nice looking and had a nice tan, and finally, that he wore no wedding ring.

He added, "I mean, they're not usually this busy on a weekday."

Alma nodded. She thought he seemed kind of awkward.

Hank said something else about shrimp and made another observation about the store and then another. Alma didn't respond but started putting her small collection of groceries on the belt. She moved to the end of the counter and carefully arranged them in her grocery bag as they were checked. She hated for her strawberries to get crushed by a can of something. When she was ready to go she turned back. "Thanks," she said, though it wasn't clear whether she was speaking to the young man or to the checker.

Alma wasn't annoyed or frightened by the man's attention. She thought, "He seems harmless, and he is good looking. He's probably OK." She put her shrimp into the refrigerator the minute she got home. She tossed them out the next day.

A week later they bumped into each other again.

Hank said, "Hey, looks like we're shopping on the same schedule, huh?"

"Oh, you're the shrimp man."

"Guess so. Actually, I'm the lobster man; I know more about lobsters than shrimp."

Alma kept her cart moving, but Hank was easily keeping up with her; he carried a small hand basket.

"Oh," was all she said.

"So, how'd you fix the shrimp?"

"Just cold, with a cocktail sauce," Alma lied. "Are you following me?"

"I guess I am. Can't hide it. I've been trying to figure out a way to ask you out."

Alma stopped and looked at him. He was good looking, as she'd noticed before. "Ask me out?" She was stalling for time.

"Yeah, how about a movie tonight? I've been wanting to see Jaws, heard it's really good and it's about fishing and all. I'd like you to go with me. My treat, of course."

She thought part of his attractiveness was his awkwardness, unlike Anthony, who'd been smooth. "Just a movie?"

He didn't fully comprehend her question. "Oh, well how about dinner first then? Then the movie?"

"No."

"OK. Let's just do the movie, OK? It starts at eight, right around the corner. I can pick you up at seven thirty and we'll get there in plenty of time."

Alma didn't like movies, but she did want to go out with this attractive awkward man.

"OK, I guess so. I'll meet you there at seven forty. And I'll buy my own ticket."

"Gee, that's great, I mean great that you'll come. But I'll be happy to pick you up. And to buy your ticket."

He seemed safe, but Alma had no intention of letting him know where she lived. "Seven forty. I'll meet you in the lobby. Now quit following me and let me finish my shopping."

"OK, OK. Great. I'll see you then." Alma was already moving away and Hank stood watching her go. "Gosh," he thought, "she's a little strange. But OK, we've got a date." He turned in the opposite direction and they didn't bump into each other again until seven forty, in the movie lobby, where Hank had been waiting for fifteen minutes and Alma arrived punctually.

Although she didn't like movies, Alma thought this was a safe way to get to know the guy.

Alma didn't enjoy Jaws. Nor the fast-food restaurant Hank persuaded her to go to after. There he discussed at length, with some passion, the accuracies and inaccuracies and ludicrocities in the film and told her how sad he was that so many people were now fishing for sharks, which he blamed on the movie.

"Ludicrocities," was the word he used and Alma liked it. And he gave good answers when she asked questions and he didn't make her feel ignorant and he clearly knew what he was talking about. Alma judged that he was sharing things that he truly cared about, not just showing off his knowledge to impress her. She judged the date a success even with the movie and fast food, mainly because she'd enjoyed his company. She rated it a solid B, maybe even a B plus, which wasn't bad, really not bad at all.

Hank preferred doing rather than reading, but he was no dummy. He was an expert in marine biology, specializing in the genetics of lobsters. It wasn't too hard to become an expert in such a limited niche. He read the few relevant books, and he kept up with the surprising number of journals related to lobsters, like *The Journal of Crustacean Biology.* There was a lot published about lobstering and of course, about genetics in general.

On their second date, Hank confessed that as far as he knew, there hadn't been any outbreak of Salmonella from Thailand shrimp and his neighbor hadn't been sick. "I was just looking for a way to connect, more than hello or talking about the store. I do know a lot about shrimp, though. You can ask me anything."

His laugh triggered a laugh from her and the date started off pleasantly, no movie this time, just a nice dinner in a quiet restaurant. Hank made an appealing suggestion that they become more intimate, much more intimate, which was very quick, yeah, and it was appealing, but Alma declined and held out until the third date.

They had sex twice, the third date and the fourth. It wasn't satisfactory for either of them and there was no more of that but they kept dating just to enjoy each other's company.

On the fifth date, Hank told Alma that he lived with his mother.

"I'd like you to meet her. You'll like each other. I'd really like that."

Alma was uneasy. She said to herself, "This is too much, too fast."

"You live with your mother?" That wasn't impressive.

"Yeah. I know it sounds strange, but when you learn a little more I think you'll understand. At least I hope so."

"Why would you want me to meet your mother?"

"Like I said, I think you'll like each other, and also you'll understand better. Please, I'd really like you to."

Alma was even more wary when she saw how much this meant to Hank, both meeting his mother and understanding. She wondered, "Am I getting too important to him? This might not be good." But she did like him, and she did enjoy his company.

"Well, I don't know. If I meet her, I don't want you to think it means something."

"What do you mean?"

"Isn't that clear? My meeting your mother is just that, me meeting her, that's all. Don't go giving it some other significance."

Hank understood from his minimal experience that he didn't understand women, but he understood what Alma was saying.

It hurt his feelings, but Alma was about to agree to meet his mother and that overrode the hurt.

"Sure, of course not. She's nice and you're nice, and you're both intelligent, I mean both of you are smarter'n me, and I think you'll both enjoy it. C'mon, give it a try, won't hurt anything and it won't mean anything, OK?"

"OK, I'll do it." And she did.

By the way, although Hank truly didn't understand women, I mean what man really does, although some gay men seem to come close, Hank was actually quite intelligent, just not in the same bookish way as Alma, or Anthony, or as it turned out, his mother.

Alma did like Hank's mother, who was friendly but not too friendly. She showed interest in Alma as much as Alma was willing to share, but didn't interrogate her. Alma learned that his mother had been in jail for civil rights protests and that she had a degree in English.

Then Alma learned that this nice woman was actually not Hank's mother. When her first husband died, she took in foster children to make ends meet; Hank was her third foster child, four years old. She fell in love with him and when she remarried she and her new husband adopted him. She and Alma agreed that he seemed a pretty adoptable kind of guy. Hank blushed.

Alma thought this was getting too heavy so she changed the subject, to books. Hank's mother was a fan of Gabriel Garcia Marquez and Jose Saramago and when Alma, who'd said she read a lot, confessed that she'd never heard of them, Hank's mother insisted on giving her a list of books. Alma promised that she'd read some of them, and over time she did. Some she didn't care for, but others she liked very much, especially *Love In the Time of Cholera* and *The Cave*.

After his mother handed her the list, Hank took Alma's hand. "Come on upstairs a minute, I want to show you something."

Alma hesitated. This felt strange. She'd read about men inviting women to "see my etchings," but with his mother sitting there, she thought it must be safe.

"Your bedroom?"

He said yes.

Alma half-turned and looked at his mother, who smiled and said, "Go ahead dear, it'll be all right."

"OK, but promise to leave the door open," Alma said half-joking. Hank and his mother laughed and Hank led her up the stairs. When he opened the bedroom door, she was blown away.

His bedroom walls were covered with beautiful photographs, mostly of lobsters. The others she couldn't figure out. Hank explained that these were from the electron microscope. He showed her the different parts of the cells and the other microparticles that the scope revealed. She asked if he'd taken the pictures and he said he had.

She asked, "All of them?"

He smiled. "Yep. All of them."

She was impressed, with the beauty of the pictures, with his skill and knowledge, and with what he was doing. Her estimation of him rose significantly. Before this, she hadn't thought much about what he did, just something with lobsters, which had sounded pretty simple.

Back downstairs, Hank said it was time to leave for dinner. Alma thanked his mother for the book suggestions and they left. On the way to the restaurant, she told Hank how much she'd liked his mother and how much she'd enjoyed their conversation.

Hank chuckled, "I knew you would."

Alma reminded him not to make anything of it and he just chuckled again.

"No, I mean it," she protested.

"OK, OK," he said, waving a hand in the air. "Don't mean nothing. Drive on," an edited version of a Vietnam war saying he'd picked up in the Marines although he'd never been in Vietnam.

"OK, then," Alma snorted. Then she pushed him until he explained the saying, and then she regretted asking.

Later, Hank tried to explain genetics to her, but Alma couldn't grasp the topic even though he kept it simple, which wasn't easy. The double helix and base pairs and genes on the chromosomes which split and you get half from each parent but in the process they intermingle and can get messed up with either too much or not enough of something and -well, it was too much for her. She stopped him and said, "Whoa, I give up. Enough!"

It was like their sex life, nonexistent now, which they'd also given up on. But there's more to life than sex, they tell me, and possibly more to life than genetics.

As Hank was driving her home after a pleasant dinner at an Italian restaurant, Alma was thinking, "I like this guy; he's nice and he's smarter than I thought. But he's coming on too strong; this is too fast. Anyway, I like his mother. I hope I'll see her again, but I don't want to get tangled up."

If you'd pointed out to Alma that she was extremely wary, she'd have understood what you meant, although she wouldn't have thought of that herself, but if you'd also pointed out that she was becoming more open and growing some, she wouldn't have appreciated your suggestion nor agreed that becoming more open was a positive thing.

But there was more growing to come.

THE LOBSTER MAN (AS ALMA CAME TO THINK OF HIM)

Hank and Alma learned more about each other. Hank shared easily and honestly. Alma shared, too, but it wasn't natural for her.

Hank knew nothing about his birth parents. As an adult he'd made a few inquiries but the records were sealed. He wasn't very disappointed; he was quite satisfied with his adoptive parents, whom he regarded as his true parents.

Hank had been an athlete and had lettered in several sports in high school. But it was a small school, and while he was good, he wasn't college-level good. In college he ran the half-mile for the freshman track team but he was the next to the slowest on the team and he didn't continue the next year.

After two years of college, Hank couldn't decide on a major so he joined the Marines. He chose the Marines because his father had been a Marine, although the choice was surprising in view of what his father had told him about The Corps. But Hank felt challenged and he wanted to measure up to his father, who he loved and admired.

Hank actually enjoyed basic training somewhat, in spite of the harassment and brutality of the drill sergeant. His father had warned him about this and Hank accepted it as part of the deal. In fact, The Corps had changed and basic wasn't as tough as he'd expected, but it was tough enough. Being an athlete helped him excel. He got an early promotion which made him proud and slightly reduced the crap he had to put up with. After basic, he went on to AIT, advanced infantry training, which wasn't as hard as basic; there was less abuse and more book learning.

Hank became ambivalent about the Marines. When he'd enlisted, he'd considered making The Corps a career, but -

Dear Mom and Dad,

Here I am in California. There's some nice scenery around if you look for it but mostly it's just a post, what can I say. Haven't had a chance to go into town yet, but I hear it's not much, I'm really not interested in loud bars and hot women, and they say the townies don't like us and you can't really make any connections.

I hope you are OK and I love getting your letters. And thanks for the chocolate chip cookies, they were great. I shared them of course and they didn't last long - hint, hint.

Dad, you were right about the sergeants, they're worse than I expected. They're all lifers and most of them couldn't make it outside The Corps. I'd guess their average IQ around ninety, plus a lot of them are drunks. You can't polish stupid. It's not so much that they abuse us, that's part of their job, but I think some of them go overboard just for kicks. I feel sorry for some of the guys that aren't too bright or in good shape. I thought they'd weeded out the weak ones in basic, but I guess it wasn't hard enough, not like when you were in, Dad. They really become targets and get way more than their share of abuse. Maybe they're trying to weed them out now, at least the ones that can't take it. We have two or three dropouts a week, even after basic. But there are a couple of sergeants I admire. One of them anyway has been in a lot of combat and sometimes he'll get us together and give us some tips, stuff that's not in the books, and he actually seems to care about us staying alive.

They made me a fire team leader so I'm responsible for three other guys. They're good kids but one of them is one of the weak ones. We help him as much as we can. He's not getting any brighter but we help him learn the stuff and he's catching on and he's lost some weight, most of us have, and he's getting stronger so I think he's gonna make it.

There's things I like about The Corps - it's so physical, and I like the structure and having a mission and the belonging, like we're all in this together. But Lord, the stupidity and rigidity. They're training us to not think, just do what the book says even when it doesn't make any sense. I'm not about to drop out, never, but I've about decided not to re-up after my four years.

Lights out. Gotta go.

Love, and thanks again for the cookies

Your Marine son, Corporal Hank, Semper Fi

It turned out that Hank's decision not to re-up was irrelevant.

The Marines and the Army were experimenting with joint exercises. Hank's AIT platoon was sent to Fort Polk, an army post in Louisiana, for a forty-eight-hour exercise. Their mission was to find and surround an army unit that was hiding in the swamps. The only rules were there was to be no physical contact between individuals and no live rounds were to be carried.

It rained the whole forty- eight hours. The sergeant in charge of the platoon was drunk the whole forty-eight hours. On the second night, the Marines came to a river in flood and the sergeant ordered them to cross. Not a good idea. The first two Marines got across but the next two slipped and fell and started to drown. Hank jumped in to help them.

Hank slipped and was being swept downriver by the strong current, but he managed to grab the collar of one of the Marines. He was holding the man's head above water when Hank's foot wedged between two rocks. He felt the bones in his ankle snap. Hank managed to keep his hold on the man's collar and eventually someone, not the sergeant who was totally ineffective, got a long tree branch and the two were pulled from the river. The other Marine who'd fallen in drowned as did a second man.

"Man"- they were both eighteen. The bodies weren't found until two days later, wedged under logs about half a mile downstream.

After the men laid Hank and his rescuee on the ground, it was obvious that Hank's leg was broken; feet don't usually stick out sideways from the leg. Several of the Marines ran up and down the river bank yelling for the two men who'd been lost, but there was no response and they saw no trace of them; they came trudging back, cursing.

The sergeant started yelling at them, probably orders, but he wasn't coherent. Two men grabbed his arms and a third one began hitting him in the stomach. Hank yelled at them to stop. The sergeant vomited and fell to the ground. He lay there moaning. The men rigged a seated stretcher from two rifles and two jackets to carry Hank. By now he was moaning softly and very pale but he never passed out. They left the sergeant on the river bank and the platoon, minus three, walked, not marched, back to the post.

Two days later a mandatory service for the two drowned Marines was held in the Fort Polk Chapel. No one noted that one of the Marines had been a passionate atheist, but they would've held the service anyway. Hank missed the event because he was still in the hospital, where his unit commander and the sergeant, the drinker, visited briefly and pinned a medal on his pajama shirt and shook his hand before the head nurse hustled them out. After they were gone, the medal made a dull clunk when Hank tossed it into his bedside waste paper basket.

The families of the two dead Marines demanded an investigation. The Corps tried to cover up. The AIT unit commander sent a letter expressing his sincere regrets. He praised the dedication and courage of their sons, and how they'd been popular and admired in their unit, although of course, he knew absolutely nothing about them except that they were dead and had parents who were damn nuisances. And they truly were nuisances; they got their congressmen involved. I should've said congresspeople, as the feistier of the two was a woman, who pushed for an investigation. So joint exercises were put on hold and the congresswoman was informed that the sergeant had been demoted. This wasn't exactly true, but it was a bit of satisfaction to the families.

The bereaved families also received a letter from the Fort Polk base commander offering his thoughts and prayers. One father replied suggesting what the base commander could do with his thoughts and prayers. The commander never would have done this, even if he'd actually read the father's letter. This letter, like all of the commander's mail, was processed by his clerk, a sergeant, the actual author of the commander's letter. Upon reading the father's letter, he had a good laugh at the expense of the commander whom he wasn't fond of, before depositing the letter in the appropriate receptacle, a receptacle quite different than the one the father had suggested for the commander's thoughts and prayers.

After the chapel service, the Marines packed up and were ready to be transported to the train station when the ex-sergeant blew his brains out with his forty-five caliber sidearm. He hadn't had the consideration to go outside, so this made a hell of a mess in the barracks and nauseated some of the enlisted men who had to clean it up. But they were Army, not nearly as tough as Marines.

We don't have the capacity, as we believe God has, to see the big picture, so we can't know for sure, but possibly those Marines who drowned were actually fortunate. Hank's platoon was soon sent to Vietnam. Many of them didn't return. There are worse ways of dying than drowning in a river in Louisiana.

Hank's broken ankle required surgery and a steel plate. The surgery was performed in the Fort Polk hospital by an army surgeon known to his colleagues as "Bumbling Bob the Bumbler." They called him "Bumble" for short. The lower ranks called him Major. But nobody ever called him "Doctor," as they did the other surgeons.

Bob hadn't been successful in civilian life. After he lost operating privileges at the third hospital in a row, he'd chosen an army career. He bungled Hank's surgery and Hank forever walked with a slight limp. He couldn't walk or stand for long periods so he was honorably discharged with a small disability pension: a small pension, a slight limp, a steel plate, chronic pain, and memories.

The pension was helpful.

The limp was barely noticeable. Alma didn't notice it until the end of their second date.

The metal plate caused some hassle with security when he flew to scientific conferences.

The pain helped him predict the weather. Hank never took anything for it; he was still a Marine.

The memories came to him in occasional nightmares.

The pain in Hank's ankle was always present, but rarely severe. It did have an effect on Hank and Alma's efforts at intimacy, although it wasn't the only factor.

After his discharge, Hank worked as a clerk in his foster uncle's shoe store for seven months. He hated it. When his father died, he had no more connection to the uncle so no job. He used his small pension to go back to college.

Hank still didn't know what he wanted to major in, but he became fascinated by a biology course. He developed a deep interest in marine biology, the field of his excellent biology professor. Unfortunately, the college didn't offer a major in that subspecialty, so he transferred to another college; otherwise, he presumably never would have met Alma, so maybe it wasn't unfortunate after all.

Alma felt for Hank. "He's had a hard life. And he's brave. A good guy." But she just said, "Hmmm" when he finished his tale. She thought, "But he's been lucky, too. He has that great relationship with an adoptive mother. Probably my childhood was worse than his. Oh, but we don't know about his first four years."

Hank and Alma went out to eat or for long walks two or three times a week. They went to no more movies after Alma revealed her dislike of them. There was no tension once they'd given up on the sexual and the genetics things.

Hank took her for her first visit to a zoo, and it was her last. She thought it was interesting but it made her uncomfortable to see the animals caged like that.

The aquarium was different. She didn't feel sorry for the fish. They had enough space and a comfortable habitat. Alma liked watching a fish as it swam around a huge tank. She'd try to figure out what it was doing and if there was any pattern to its movement. She'd wonder what it was thinking, or if it was just acting on instinct.

Alma also liked the schools of smaller fish. So beautiful and graceful, they reminded her of ballet. She'd seen two ballets with Anthony and she'd said they were beautiful but two were enough for her.

Hank's work fascinated him and he was usually engrossed in it, but he was thinking more and more about Alma. He wished he could explain his work to her in a way she'd understand, but it was highly technical and anyone would need at least a couple of courses in genetics to have any chance of understanding it. He'd done his best to explain it in simple terms, and she did her best to understand, but it was just frustrating for both of them.

Hank did a lot of scuba diving in his work, and he offered to teach Alma but she declined. Months later she finally told him that she'd never learned to swim. After all, when would she have?

In the fall, they were walking back from a pleasant dinner at an Italian restaurant and it started to drizzle. Hank took Alma's hand. Suddenly he said, "I think I love you."

Alma was startled. She blurted out, "What?" and stopped in her tracks.

Hank turned to face her. "I love you."

Alma frowned and was silent. Then she and said, "Oh, Hank. Really. It's too early, too soon. You don't know me. Let's hurry and get in before it really starts to rain."

Hank said, "OK" and let go of her hand. They started walking again, faster now.

Alma was right. It did start to rain hard. And if Hank had known her better, he never would've used the L word.

He never tried it again.

One Saturday afternoon Hank was drawn to his mother's kitchen by the smell of baking. He would've been out on the water but it was too windy. He was thinking about Alma.

"She's intelligent and I sure enjoy being with her. But she's kind of, I wouldn't say cold, distant maybe. She's not as fond of me as I am of her. Actually, I'm not sure she's fond of me at all, but she must enjoy my company at least." He chuckled to himself, "I know it's not cause she's after my money. I wish we could make the sex thing work, but it is what it is. Would that change if we could get closer? I wish I could figure out how to reach her, how to make things better between us."

You may be wondering exactly what the sex problem was, why neither one of them enjoyed it. No offense intended, but I wonder why you wonder? Do you need to know those intimate details? Don't you think Alma and Hank might feel some shame around that issue and would appreciate some privacy?

OK, if you really must know, it was a mixture of physical, emotional, and psychological issues that prevented success, and that's all I know about it, and honestly, all I care to know. So let's just move on, shall we?

In his mind, Hank was having this dialogue with his mother, explaining the situation to her and wanting her advice, but he never actually had that conversation. He was just sitting staring into his cup of coffee, which had gone cold quite a while ago.

"Hey, where are you?" his mother asked. "You've drifted off. Are you OK?"

"Huh? Oh, yeah; I'm fine. Fine. Sure smells good in here."

His mother was paying close attention to her baking but she was very sensitive to Hank and his moods.

"What're you thinking about, besides cookies?"

He hadn't known what she was baking until then, but the idea excited him.

"Wow, I hope they're chocolate chip?"

"Wait and see. Anyway, what's got you so preoccupied? It's not like you."

"Nothing, really. I was just thinking about Alma."

"You got girl problems?"

"No, not really. Not problems. I just wish I understood her better, that's all."

"What do you mean? Can you tell me more?"

Hank was silent for a minute and then he sighed and pushed away his coffee cup.

"Nope, that's it. Just wishing. It'll be OK. How about those cookies, are they ready yet?"

His mother knew she'd gone as far as she could. She shook her head and let it go.

"Yep, here you go. Chocolate chip, your favorites. Careful, they're hot. Maybe they'll make you feel better. Don't spoil your dinner now."

"OK. Chocolate chip. Yes!" and he grabbed three off the plateful his mother had set on the table. Actually, they did make him feel a little better; chocolate can do that, at least for a while.

You and I might think a real dialog with his mother would've been a good idea, probably leaving out the sex part. His mother might've suggested that with Alma it wasn't so much what he needed to do, but what he needed to not do, and that he needed to have patience, a lot of patience. But I guess pride kept him from asking his mother, and possibly he was afraid of what she might say if he did. And anyway, he was a man, and you know how they are.

So Hank kept ruminating and wishing. At one point, he was so distracted from his work that he nearly ruined an experiment by not watching the time, but fortunately, he caught himself and the experiment turned out OK. But he did need to focus, and Alma wasn't helping him with that.

A few months later, Hank messed up again, messed up with Alma, not on his work; he didn't slip up on that again, although his focus still wasn't what it should've been.

The weather was pleasant and they were strolling along on a walk.

"You know Alma, I've been thinking."

"Hhhmmm?"

"Well, it's nice living with my mom. She's wonderful, makes it easy, but what if I moved out? I could get a place, you could help me pick it, and you could move in with me. I'd love for us to live together."

He made the mistake of using the L word again, although in a different sense. Still, it caused Alma a momentary discomfort, but she wouldn't have liked the suggestion anyway.

"Oh, no, I don't think so. Aren't we doing fine like we are? Isn't this going OK?"

"Yeah, sure, I'm not complaining, it's great, but I think it'd really be nice if we lived together. Maybe we could just try it for a while?"

"No, I don't think that's a good idea. I'm happy where I am and we're having a good time. Let's just keep enjoying this."

Hank didn't get it; he pushed. He really should've had that conversation with his mother. "Well, couldn't you even consider it? Think about it for a while before you say?"

"No!"

Alma saw that Hank looked hurt, but she didn't say anything more and he dropped it. That seemed like the end of it, but Alma didn't forget the conversation.

They finished their stroll and Hank kissed her goodnight. She didn't invite him in. That was only slightly unusual and maybe it didn't mean anything. Maybe.

They had a few more dates, pleasant, no different than before. But Alma was uncomfortable. She was thinking, "Uh oh, I'm getting too attached to Hank and he's sure attached to me. Watch out." Then she thought, "The longer this goes on, it's just gonna be harder to end it. And it's too soon after Anthony for another relationship."

Maybe the breakup with Anthony had bothered her more than she'd realized?

"I like Hank, a lot. He's a nice guy, smart, educated. He doesn't read much, not my kind of books anyway, but that's not the point. Somehow he's just not right for me. I enjoy him, but it isn't clicking. I need to end it now before it goes any further. That'll be better for both of us."

Alma didn't give much thought to how to tell Hank. After coffee, in another unremarkable restaurant, she just said it.

"Hank, this isn't working."

His head jerked up and his eyes were big.

"What do you mean?"

"Don't you see this isn't working? We just don't click. It's time we stopped."

"No, I don't see that it's not working. Let's just give it time. Give it a chance. Is it the sex?"

"Oh my God, no!" Alma hardly ever used the G word, but this just came out.

She thought a second. "Well, maybe a little. But that's not really it."

"Have I done something wrong?"

"No. No. I like you a lot. You're a very nice person. I enjoy you. But it doesn't click. It isn't there. If we wait longer, it'll just hurt more and I don't want to hurt you. Or myself either."

Hank kept pushing; he couldn't help himself.

"Come on, Alma. You're a special person. I don't want to lose you. I want us to keep on. Let's give it a try."

He reached across the table and put his hand on hers but she pulled away.

"No. I'm getting a cab. I don't want to see you again."

Alma was pained to see tears in his eyes.

Hank asked if he could call her.

She said no.

And that was that. Well, nearly.

Hank's mother knew something wasn't right as soon as she heard him come in. He didn't slam the door, but he closed it harder than usual. And he was home early. He came into the room and the look on his face confirmed her intuition.

"Sonny. What's wrong?"

"Damn," he replied, not really much of an answer.

"What's wrong??"

"Alma just broke up with me. Damn!"

"Oh my! What happened?"

"Nothing happened. She just said that's it; she doesn't want to see me again."

"Oh my. What had you done? Or what hadn't you done? It wouldn't have just happened."

Hank's mother was sitting on the sofa, enjoying *The Living*, a novel by Annie Dillard, who doesn't usually write novels. She carefully put a bookmark in the book and closed it. She treasured books and never would put one face down or turn down a corner, even in this moment of stress. She laid the book on the small table to her right. She patted the sofa near her for Hank to sit down but he kept standing and then he started pacing.

"Nothing happened. Nothing at all. She just said it wasn't gonna work and it was better to break it off now. I don't understand her. I'll never understand women."

"Well, of course not. You're a man. There wasn't anything to trigger this? Nothing else happened?"

"No. No."

"Well, I'm sorry. I liked Alma, but what do you know about her?"

"Well, you know her. She's smart, and good looking, and rich, I suppose. And she likes to read. She's read some of those books you suggested."

"And after, what is it, eight, nine months, that's all you know about her?"

"Yep. I liked her a lot. I thought we were doing fine.

"Well, if that's all you know about her, does that tell you something?"

"What do you mean?"

"Do you know anything about her family or her friends?"

Hank frowned. "No, she doesn't talk much about her family. And I don't know that she has any friends."

"OK, I don't want to psychoanalyze, but after all this time, you don't know anything about her, not anything really. How does that add up to you?"

"I don't know. I really like her."

"I know. I know. But she sounds closed up."

"Closed up?"

"Not open. Maybe not open to relationships. You really like her. Could that've scared her? Or what if she really liked you?"

Hank didn't understand women but he wasn't dumb. "Like we were getting too close or something?"

"You think? Had you been pushing a little?"

Hank stopped pacing. He rubbed his chin. "Yeah, I guess, maybe a little." His ankle was hurting more than usual but he ignored it.

"Well, maybe she's been hurt and she's scared of getting hurt again. Maybe she was starting to like you and that spooked her. Does that make any sense?"

Hank's mother had majored in English, not psychology, but she was smart, and novels can give you some insights into human behavior. And she was a woman.

Hank finally sat down on the sofa. His mother reached over and patted his hand. He rubbed his ankle slowly.

"You know," he said, "I think I'll send her some flowers. What do you think?"

"I think you might as well save your money. Didn't you say you'd been pushing? And Alma seems like a woman who knows her mind. If she says it's over, maybe it's over."

"Well, I'm going to call her."

"I wouldn't do that either if I was you."

"Well, I have to try something. I can't just let this go."

His mother sighed. "I'm so sorry; I know this really hurts, but I don't think there's much you can do. They say, `Never chase a runner.'" She reached to pat his hand again but he was already at the telephone.

Alma let the phone ring four times before she picked it up. She said nothing. She'd thought he might call.

"Hello?"

Silence

"Hello."

Silence

"Alma. Are you there? Hello? Are you there?"

Alma hung up, gently.

Hank got the message.

It was only later that night after he was in bed that he cried, but only for a few minutes. Marines don't cry.

He didn't send flowers and he didn't call again

Alma changed markets. She didn't want to bump into Hank. Unbeknownst to her, so did Hank but his new market wasn't the same as hers.

And that was truly that.

After that, life was uneventful. Again.

For a while.

ALMAS'S BROKEN LEG

For the next two years, Alma had no dates. She wasn't bad looking, really not bad looking at all, but she had a way of carrying herself that said she didn't want to be bothered and this was mostly effective. She had only a few offers, which she courteously declined. She didn't need to be rude or crude, just firm.

"Thank you, no. I'm not dating. But thank you anyway."

"Oh, it wouldn't have to be a date. We could just take a walk or share dinner. Or just coffee and a dessert. Whatever you'd like."

"Thank you, no. No."

Alma said to herself, "Not interested. I like my life just like it is, don't need any complications. `A woman without a man is like a fish without a bicycle.' Where did I read that?" She finally admitted to herself that while the break up with Hank hadn't been nearly as painful for her as was for Hank, it had been painful enough. "I don't want to go through that again."

But after two pleasant years, Alma felt restless, like she needed something more in her life, like something was missing. Some people might think this suggested a spiritual yearning, a need for a connection to something larger than herself, but that idea never entered Alma's mind, and if it had, she would've quickly rejected it. Alma didn't want to be dependent on any man, and certainly not on a God, or a god, whom most people thought of as He, a male, which seemed ridiculous to her on the few occasions that she briefly had any thought about it.

Or some people might think that the feeling was simply loneliness. If you'd suggested this to Alma, she certainly would have denied it and probably would've been insulted.

I can imagine her saying, "Lonely? Are you kidding? I've never been lonely. I'm independent. I might enjoy company, intelligent conversation, but I don't need it. No, I'm not lonely, not a bit, thank you very much."

If you'd heard this, you might've thought she's protesting too much, to use a cliché, but if you're smart you wouldn't have said that to Alma. You would've just dropped it right there, as we will now.

Alma needed a change. She decided to sell the coffee shop and do something else. She offered the shop to Arnid, who was still the manager. She liked the young woman and thought she did a fine job of managing, but that didn't affect the high price Alma held out for. Arnid got the other employees to chip in and buy shares. They were helped by Alma's generous salary. Arnid wisely kept fifty-one percent, which left her in control.

Alma still liked to drop in and chat with Arnid. She wasn't expecting the feeling of relief she got after she sold the shop. She hadn't realized she'd felt burdened by owning it. She'd been looking over Arnid's shoulder but carefully, so Arnid never felt intruded on. But as the owner, she'd felt some responsibility for the shop, for its quality and for the employees. Still, I don't think this sense of burden had much to do with her restlessness or her decision to sell the shop. And apparently her becoming aware of this feeling didn't affect her next decision.

A few months later Alma bought a high class dress boutique at a reasonable price. She closed it for two months while she supervised renovations, reopened it with a new manager, and sold it eight months later for a big, no, a huge, profit. It had been something to do, to occupy her mind and her time, but she didn't really want to own a business.

She briefly considered going into real estate. She knew she'd excel at it. She read a few books on the business and dropped the idea. It required spending too much time with other people and putting up with too much crap.

Alma faithfully continued her four a week gym sessions and her walking except in the worst weather. Life was pleasant, comfortable, but still not fulfilling, and she didn't know why.

Then something happened.

That winter on a walk she slipped and fell on the ice. The pain wasn't bad, but she knew that her leg was broken. She tried to get up but couldn't. Fortunately, she'd dressed warmly and she'd fallen onto some wet leaves and not into the dirty snow on the side of the path and the pain wasn't bad. Alma thought maybe the cold helped keep the pain down.

She wasn't frightened, just annoyed at the inconvenience. She had things planned for the afternoon and it looked like those weren't going to happen, not today. The path she routinely used was popular and soon enough a young couple came by with their medium-sized dog. The couple was chatting and the dog saw Alma first and began straining on his leash to get to her. When he got near, Alma had the fleeting thought that he might pee on her but he started licking her face, which was nearly as bad. The man quickly pulled him away, yelling "Roger! No! Down! Down!" which the dog totally ignored, continuing to strain to get to her but now restrained at a more comfortable distance.

Alma told the couple that she needed help, which was, of course, obvious and the woman already had her cell phone out, only waiting to be sure Alma wasn't just drunk before she called 911. The couple nicely waited with her and even kept Roger off except for a few moments when they were distracted by another couple that wandered by and wanted an explanation of what was going on.

They left Alma lying where she was because they didn't know what might be broken and they didn't want to take the chance of causing more damage, bad for Alma and possibly exposing them to a lawsuit. Alma agreed that that was the wisest course. The man offered to put his jacket over her, but Alma thanked him and said she wasn't cold, which wasn't entirely truthful. He was just as glad.

Alma thought that waiting twenty minutes for an ambulance was a little much, but that maybe gunshots and car wrecks took precedence over a broken leg so she didn't complain when the ambulance arrived. Besides, she thought it wiser not to risk pissing off the ambulance guys in whose hands she now was. She tried to thank the kind couple but was interrupted by the attendants with questions and examination. The couple waved and walked off, Roger leading the way, with their good Samaritan duty fulfilled and, Alma supposed, feeling pleased with themselves.

The attendants seemed to know what they were doing. They splinted her leg and checked that she could feel and move all her limbs except the broken one, where they only checked the digits. Alma liked that the lady attendant was in charge. They hoisted her onto a stretcher, into the ambulance, and were off. Alma thought she might be disappointed that they didn't use the siren but quickly realized that she didn't really care.

The leg was starting to hurt and she was trying not to move it or let it bounce and wishing they'd get to the hospital soon. She was starting to want something for pain and wasn't thinking about much else. It was her left leg, by the way, and turned out to have two breaks, but clean and not displaced thank goodness (not `thank God', who Alma, if she'd thought about it at all, wouldn't have said had anything to do with it, or with anything else for that matter).

Alma was wheeled into the emergency room. She knew nothing about hospitals. She'd never been in one before and she didn't watch TV or movies and had no interest in medical things. It's strange that nothing had come up in her fiction reading, but maybe it had and she just didn't remember it? So she had trouble understanding what was going on. The lady attendant spoke to a woman in green clothes for a moment, but Alma couldn't hear them. The place was crowded, busy and noisy, with lots of people rushing about, most dressed in green. The woman in green, who was of course a nurse, pulled the sheet off of Alma's feet and felt them, and then spoke to the attendant. She didn't put the sheet back. By this time another stretcher had come in the door and the nurse moved back to it and the attendant wheeled Alma further into the hall. Alma heard some moaning coming from that direction but she couldn't see anything; she assumed it was the latest arrival. The attendant wheeled her further down the hall and next to an empty cart.

"We're going to lift you onto this cart now," the lady said. "You don't do anything; let us do the work, OK?"

Alma made a small moan herself. "My leg hurts. Can I get something for that before you move me?"

"That'll have to be the doctor. He'll come check you soon. OK, real still now. One, two, THREE."

And Alma was on the other cart and the jostling hadn't been too bad.

The attendant patted her arm and took off the sheet which belonged to the ambulance, but left their splint on. "You take care now." The attendants moved off. The inflatable splints weren't expensive although when the ambulance bill came you would've thought they were.

"I'm cold," said Alma, but they were already too far off to hear her.

She lay there hurting and shivering for what she guessed was twenty minutes but in fact was only nine. Finally she reached out and touched a green clad man on the arm as he passed by. "Excuse me?"

He glanced at her but kept walking. He was carrying a bag of what looked like blood. It was. He seemed in a hurry. He was.

Alma was hurting, cold, and frustrated. When the next person passed close by she grabbed his green sleeve and exclaimed, "Hey, stop. Wait a minute."

He wasn't carrying anything and didn't seem in such a hurry and Alma had a good grip on his sleeve and he did stop. "What's up, lady?"

"My leg hurts and I'm cold and I've been waiting here and nobody's seen me."

"Yep, we're really busy, way behind. Somebody'll be with you soon. They know you're here."

They did. Nobody had talked to her and they didn't know her name, but unbeknownst to Alma, she'd been entered on the big green chalk board behind the main desk, as "F, L leg fx, stable. Hall cart. Level 3."

The "Level 3" explains why Alma hadn't been seen yet. She couldn't see the board and wouldn't have understood it if she had. The ones and twos on the board meant a number of people were going to be seen ahead of her, a mere three, no matter what order people had come in. And pity the fours and fives, who made up nearly half of the entrees.

The man in green obviously wanted to move on but Alma had a firm grip on his shirt. "Well, could you at least get me a sheet please?"

"Sure, I'll be right back." Alma let go and he moved on, moving faster now. He wasn't right back. Alma never saw him again.

But soon a lady in street clothes came, carrying a clipboard. She asked Alma her name and then about insurance. Alma interrupted her. "Could you please at least get me a sheet? I'm very cold."

"Oh, sure. Just a sec." And in a minute she indeed was back with not one but two sheets, and she nicely covered Alma with them. "OK, now where were we?"

Shortly after this interview, two greenies came up, who Alma guessed were a nurse and a doctor although neither introduced themselves. They both looked tired. The doctor, who also looked very young, asked about pain and allergies, and then gave an order to the nurse, who soon returned with two pills and a paper cup of water. Meanwhile, the doctor pulled the sheets off Alma's feet and felt them. Alma had no idea why these people kept after her feet. She wondered if maybe she'd fallen into a cult of foot fetishers. Of course, they were checking to make sure that her blood supply was OK; that it hadn't been interrupted by the fracture (or "fx", as the note on the green board indicated).

The doc gently felt her leg. "Seems OK. We'll get an X-ray just to make sure. Then we get you in a cast and you'll be on your way." He covered her feet back up, for which Alma was grateful.

Soon two men in green walked up and started wheeling her away. She asked, "Where are we going?"

One said, "Just around the corner," as though that answered her question but then the other said, "It's just X-ray." They left her in the hall and she lay there for slightly under an hour. Again, she wondered if anyone was aware that she was there, but mercifully after two pills the pain was minimal and she dozed much of the time. She was wakened briefly by someone's loud wailing, but it died off quickly as the wailer apparently was moved to another area or something. Alma dozed off again. Then another greeny came out of a room and called her name and Alma waved her hand in the air. "Me. I'm here. I'm Alma."

This greeny wheeled her into a room with a big table and some device hanging from the ceiling which Alma assumed was an X-ray machine, never having seen one. Another greeny appeared and the two lifted Alma onto the big table; the table was cold but they let her keep the sheets.

The second greeny left. The first put a pillow under Alma's head and left. Then her voice came from the ceiling.

"Hold still now, and when I say stop, hold your breath and don't move."

In a minute the voice said, "Hold now." Alma assumed this was as good as `stop' and so she did. There was a buzz.

Soon the greeny reappeared. Alma assumed she could breathe again and so she took a deep breath and no one complained; she couldn't have held it much longer.

Greeny said, "That should do it."

Two more greenies came, lifted her onto another cart, and wheeled her back around the corner to the emergency room. They left her in the hall against the wall.

Soon, someone, a nurse Alma guessed, appeared. "Doc says it's all OK. We'll get the cast on now."

She and another greeny with white paste adorning his outfit wheeled Alma into a small room where the pasty greeny said, "I'll put your cast on in here."

He wrapped her leg with gauze and then put plaster on it. When done, he stepped back and said, "A thing of beauty is a joy forever." And he laughed. "Now you be still and give it a chance to dry. I'll be back in ten."

And he was. He tapped on the cast, pronounced it "fine" and left. Before long, the nurse returned. Alma signed some papers for her without knowing what they were. The nurse told her to keep the cast dry, gave her some crutches and helped her off the table and into a wheelchair. "Is somebody here to drive you home? You can't drive yourself."

"No. I'll need a cab."

"I'll call you one. They're usually pretty fast. Let's get you to the front."

She placed Alma's crutches across the arms of the chair and wheeled her near the ER entrance. Soon after she left an older man in khakis came in the door. He yelled, "Cab." Alma waved at him and yelled, "Here. Here."

A greeny appeared and wheeled Alma to the cab parked at the entrance. He helped her into the cab while the cabby held the door. He laid the crutches across her lap. "Take care, now," he said. "Keep her dry," and closed the door.

The cabby got in, "Where to, lady?" and he started off without waiting for her answer or asking any more questions.

Alma had no way of knowing that her next ER visit, years away yet, would still be cold, but otherwise, would be quite different.

This emergency room experience had been about what you'd expect but it was all new to Alma. And soon enough, well, not really soon enough, but you know how those things go, Alma was back home. She hated having to use crutches, and worse, they didn't seem the right size. She hated her cast and her leg was already itching. She appreciated her bottle of pain pills.

The cabby had been nice; he'd helped her into the house and didn't mind waiting while she found her purse.

While she was crutching around she had the thought that the cabby might be casing the place or might even rob her then and there. But she thought, "That's silly. He knows I could recognize him and he'd have to kill me. And that would be going too far." She quit worrying about it and gave him a nice tip. He thanked her and left, closing the front door gently, the sound reminding her of Anthony's leaving, which she had no wish to think about.

Alma sat on the sofa for a minute, rejected the idea of wine, took one of the six pain pills they'd given her and went to bed. She slept well, as usual, but she had some weird dreams, probably due to the pill. Fortunately she didn't remember any of the details the next morning.

Well, actually she did remember seeing Anthony standing in her living room and telling some people, she had no idea who they were, "Get the hell out of here!" They just looked at him and he yelled, "I said get out now!" and they vanished, and so did he.

In her dream Alma was uncomfortable and she was uncomfortable remembering it so she quickly began planning her day and dumped the memory of the dream.

If you'd asked Alma what she thought her dream meant, she'd have looked at you with a blank stare. She wouldn't have understood the question. Yes, by this time she'd read some psychology and even some Freud, but she never imagined that any of it might apply to her. She preferred to think about things that followed logical rules, like numbers, which you could add and subtract, and with skill and luck, sometimes multiply.

Ten days later Alma fished in her purse for the appointment card from the emergency room visit. She only remembered a few things from the visit - the cold, and somebody, the nurse, the doctor, or whoever it was, saying, "You'll need to come back to the clinic in two weeks," and the card.

Alma had said she'd rather go to a private doctor. The person snorted, and then laughed out loud.

"In this town, it takes two months to get to see an orthopod. By then, this'll all be over if it goes right."

Alma wondered if they were just needing business at the clinic but the hospital seemed busy and she doubted it.

"Well, let me try anyway."

She dreaded the thought of a clinic, although she'd never actually been in one.

"OK, honey," - so it probably wasn't a doctor - "if that's what you want. But let me give you the appointment anyway just in case, OK?"

Alma thought that was a good idea and she took the card. She called two private offices and learned that the person had told her the truth. One appointment offered was in two months and the other was, "How about never?" or words to that effect, because the doctor was leaving on vacation for six weeks and when he came back he was booked for the next three months. Alma's name carried no weight and she didn't think offering a bribe was a good idea.

She called the clinic and confirmed her appointment just to be sure.

Alma became proficient on the wrong-sized crutches. She hated them but she used them conscientiously because she didn't want to take any chances of messing up her cast or her leg. And she kept the cast dry. She never got used to the itching; she just endured it. And in the back of her mind was that comment, "If it goes right." Until that moment, it had never occurred to her that it might not `go right,' whatever that meant.

Her cab arrived promptly. The cabby wasn't very communicative. That was fine with Alma, and it didn't matter much because with his thick accent she couldn't understand anything he said. He must've been experienced because he drove right to the clinic entrance. He helped Alma and her crutches out and she gave him a nice tip.

The clinic wasn't as bad as she'd feared, not quite. It wasn't too dingy or dirty. The waiting room was nearly full; some of the people looked poor, some middle class, and a few looked well off, probably not as well off as she was, although you never could tell for sure. They'd probably also been told two months for a private doctor. The one homeless guy was sitting in a corner talking to himself, but he looked old and harmless, unless he had a weapon. Still, Alma picked a chair on the other side of the room.

When her appointment time came, and went, and was long gone, Alma, who'd never been in a clinic before, went to the desk and asked the clerk about it.

"Honey, look around you. Half the people here are ahead of you. The doctors are busy, doing the best they can. Why don't you get a nice magazine and wait your turn and we'll call you, OK?"

The lady continued smacking her gum during this monologue and never looked up from her computer. Alma couldn't see the screen and could only imagine what might be on there.

"Thanks, I'll do that."

Alma realized that the woman was holding all the cards and confrontation could make things worse. She considered walking out but she'd already waited that long and private wasn't an option, so she might as well stick it out. She'd seen that the magazines were dirty and wrinkled and none of them would've interested her anyway, so she just sat. And sat. And eventually was indeed called.

She was seen by a man in green scrubs and a white jacket with no identification on it and a stethoscope sticking out of the pocket. He never introduced himself so she had no idea who or what he was. He could have been a tech, or a physician's assistant, a nurse, or a doctor. Or even a janitor, she guessed. It only took a minute to check her cast and her toes. He said, "Looks OK," tapped twice on the cast, filled out a form, gave it to her, and then she was finally sent to X-ray. After all the time wasted sitting in the waiting room. Alma was irritated, an emotion she was capable of being aware of.

The wait in X-ray was mercifully short; she wondered why when so many people were sitting in the clinic waiting room, but she was grateful. The X-ray tech was courteous, efficient, and disinterested and soon Alma was back in the waiting room. A half-hour later she was called into the exam room and soon the doctor came in. She knew he was the doctor because he did introduce himself. He was a middle-aged man with a nice smile and a gentle unhurried manner. She liked him at once.

"How'd this happen to you?" he asked and she described the accident.

"From one to ten, what's your pain level today?"

"Close to zero, I guess." She did actually have an occasional twinge, especially at night when she was wanting to sleep, but the itch was worse than the pain and Alma, being stoic, didn't think it worth mentioning.

"Good, good." He smiled, patted her cast and felt her toes. He put the X-ray he'd brought in with him up on a lightbox; Alma assumed it was hers. He pointed out the breaks on the two bones which even Alma could see.

"Could've been a lot worse," he observed. Smiling at her again, he said "Everything looks good. I expect you're going to be just fine. Keep using the crutches and in two weeks we'll take that cast off and put you in a walking boot."

After she'd managed to forget the "If it goes right" comment, Alma had never imagined anything different from being just fine and his "I expect" frightened her a bit. Still, his manner was calming and reassuring. Then he smiled at her again and said, "Can I ask you something?"

The question puzzled her. He was the doctor after all.

"OK?" she ventured.

"I'm not supposed to do this, but I was wondering, would you go out with me for a drink and maybe a snack?"

Alma was startled and she blurted out, "If you're not supposed to do this, why are you doing it?"

The nice smile again. "Well, it's strange. There's just something about you that appeals to me and I feel like I've seen you before somewhere, but I doubt it."

Alma thought for a minute. She liked him and he was a doctor, so he was probably OK, and she was at loose ends.

"I don't know. Let me think about it."

"Sure. Can I call you?"

She nodded yes, still feeling a little confused.

He pulled a prescription pad out of his white jacket pocket, gave her a blank and asked her to write her phone number on the back. When she handed the paper back with her number, he folded it and stuck it in his jacket pocket.

"Good. I'll give you a call."

She nodded yes again, thanked him for his help and crutched her way back to the desk. The clerk was still at her computer, still smacking. She looked up this time, gave Alma an appointment slip for two weeks and turned back to her computer without saying goodbye, thank you, or go screw yourself.

Alma took a cab home, picked up the book she was halfway through and didn't think any more about the experience.

Two weeks later, she went back to the clinic and dealt with, or was dealt with by, the same receptionist, smacking what Alma thought might be the same wad of gum. The cast was easily removed by the same nameless tech and he started to put on a walking boot.

"Wait! Hold on a minute." Alma sighed in relief as she finally scratched her leg. It had been itching for two weeks.

The tech frowned impatiently but then he sighed, "OK, wait a minute. That scratching'll only make it worse." He opened a drawer and handed her a tube of moisturizing cream. "Here. Use this."

She put some on and it was soothing but she still had to resist the urge to scratch. The tech put on the boot and told her not to get it wet. He explained how she could remove it herself in two weeks and she wouldn't need another appointment. Fine with her. Then he picked up the crutches and left the room, just like that.

On her way out of the clinic, she was passed by the nice doctor who was hurrying to another exam room, chart in hand. He stopped when he saw her, gave her that nice smile, waved and moved on. Alma smiled back. On the way out, she smiled and waved at the receptionist, just out of spite although the receptionist was still looking at the computer and never noticed.

Alma went home and she forgot about the doctor.

ALMA'S UNPLEASANT DATE WITH THE DOCTOR AND ITS SURPRISING AFTERMATH

Three days after the clinic, Alma was reading a Saramago novel when the doctor called.

"Hello. Do you remember me? From the clinic?"

"Yes."

"Well, have you been thinking about my question?"

She was honest. "Not really."

"Oh." Pause. "Well, would you think about it now?"

"OK."

"Here's the deal. My brother and I have tickets to a Judy Collins concert on Tuesday and he's bringing his girlfriend. We can all go out for drinks and dinner and then to the concert. We won't be getting home too late; I'm working Wednesday. Do you like Judy Collins?"

"I don't know. I've never heard of her."

Judy Collins hadn't been in Anthony's CD collection, at least not in the ones she'd ever heard.

"Oh." Pause. "Well, would you give it a try? I'd really like that."

Now it was her turn to pause. She could hear his breathing over the phone. It sounded calm and steady.

"OK, I'll give it a try."

Arrangements were made; he told her to dress casual. She figured that meant slacks were OK. The doctor picked her up at the appointed time. He looked nice and he didn't bring flowers, as she'd feared he might. He greeted her in a friendly way, said she looked nice, and escorted her out to the Lexus where she met his brother Brad and Brad's girlfriend, Jillian. She liked Brad right off, as she had the doctor, but she wasn't sure about Jillian, whose warm greeting seemed a little excessive and phony. Just a feeling.

On the drive to a nearby restaurant, they mostly discussed the concert. They apparently all knew this Judy Collins person and had been to her concerts before. Alma felt left out although they courteously tried to include her as best they could.

The restaurant was nice, but not extravagant. The doctor gave the car keys to the valet, who held the doors for Alma and Jillian, and the doctor held the restaurant door for them all. When they were shown to a lousy table, right by the door and in traffic, he quickly got them a better one. Alma wasn't sure how he'd done that.

They settled in at the better table and ordered drinks. The doctor ordered a martini, extra dry, no olive. Brad ordered a beer and Jillian some exotic mixed drink which sounded disgusting to Alma, who ordered white wine.

The conversation was pleasant and relaxed, roaming over various topics, their work, politics -they all sounded moderately liberal, except for Alma who had no opinion at all - and the stock market. Alma managed to participate without actually contributing or revealing much, partly because she was unfamiliar with some of the topics, partly because she didn't want to show off what she knew about the stock market, and partly because that was just her way. She wasn't ready to share herself with these strangers yet.

The doctor ordered a second round of drinks but Alma declined with a wave of her hand. She hadn't finished her first one yet. The wine was good enough and cold the way she liked it; she just always drank slowly. They ordered dinner at the same time. The doctor ordered a steak, rare, and Alma ordered a Caesar salad. She didn't notice what the other two ordered.

At that point, the doctor, without looking at her, casually put his hand on her thigh under the table. Without looking at him, she casually removed it. After a few minutes, he put it back. Alma picked up her dinner fork and plunged it into the back of his hand. She could still hear him swearing as she reached the maître de at the front door and asked for a cab. She waited outside. No one came out to say anything to her. Alma thought she should hope that she hadn't done any lasting damage to his hand, especially since he was a surgeon, but in fact, she didn't care much one way or the other. She was ready to go home and was glad when the cab came quickly. She hadn't been that hungry anyway.

Four days later she got an unexpected call from Brad. He wanted to apologize for his brother's behavior. He said he thought the doctor had already had a few drinks before he'd picked Jillian and him up, and that he really was a nice guy but that when he drank too much sometimes things got out of hand. Then he caught himself and said, "Sorry, no pun intended."

Alma said that was alright, no offense. She didn't respond to the apology, just thanked him for calling, said "Goodbye" and hung up. And that was that. Or so she thought.

Alma was better at reading women than at reading men.

So she was surprised again when she got another call from Brad. This time he never mentioned his brother, but said he just wanted to check in and see how she was doing.

"Fine," she said.

"Well, what are you doing?"

"Reading," she answered, and although she'd given him no encouragement, he asked about the book. Brad said he hadn't read it but he'd read another one by the same author and wasn't sure whether he liked it or not because while it was interesting, he couldn't understand parts of it and he couldn't figure out what the author was getting at.

"Oh," Alma said. She thought, "OK, books. But could he be fishing to set up a lawsuit over the fork? C'mon, probably not." She kept responding to Brad but only in monosyllables. She didn't want to be crude, or to rudely hang up on him, but she thought he'd catch on eventually, and he did.

"Well, nice to talk with you. Glad you're doing fine. You take care now."

And that was that.

Well, no. He called again five days later.

"Hey, how you doing?"

"What's this about?"

"What do you mean?"

"Why do you keep calling me like this?"

"Oh." Pause.

Long pause.

"Well?" she insisted.

"Well, OK, since you put it like that. OK, I liked you from the minute I saw you coming out to the car, something about the way you carry yourself, and just to be clear, there never was anything with Jillian. She might've thought so, but I never said anything to give her that impression and she's history now. And I was so impressed with the way you handled yourself in the restaurant. When you stuck him with that fork I nearly stood up and cheered. He deserved it, had for a long time. He thinks because he's a doctor he can get away with stuff. And I've been thinking about you ever since and so I decided to call, so that's it. Oh, and I kinda exaggerated when I told you he's a nice guy."

He was almost out of breath and he'd said it all and he thought he might have said too much and so he stopped.

Alma said nothing.

"Well?" he asked.

"Well, what?"

"Do you think we could get together for a cup of coffee or something?"

"No."

"Oh. Well, will you think about it?"

"No."

Oh. Well, is it OK if I call you again?"

"No."

"Oh." Pause.

"Well, I'm disappointed." Pause. "And I'm sorry." He didn't specify what he was sorry for.

Pause.

Then Alma said, "OK."

"OK, what?" Brad asked.

"OK, nothing. And please don't call again."

And she hung up.

But he did.

Alma had no idea that another chapter of her life was beginning, and there wouldn't have been much she could've done about it if she had. None of us have as much free choice or control as we imagine, but life is based on illusions or we couldn't survive as long as we do. Without our illusions we'd just fold it up and toss it away. What illusions are we talking about here, you may be wondering. The illusion of control, of course. And I'll give you a longer list later on, if you think you can stand reading it, but for now, let's just follow Alma as she enters her new phase.

But first, let me just say that I'd never intended to go into that philosophical illusion-of-control diatribe here, but something about Alma's situation pushed my button and I just did it. So there it is and I hope it didn't bore you or make you uncomfortable. But I never intended to go into that and I did it anyway. So you see, that makes my point, doesn't it? About our illusion of control? Just saying.

We left Alma not knowing that she was going to receive yet another call from Brad, the doctor's brother, who it turns out is going to be a significant character after all.

The next call was unexpected again.

Alma set her book down and answered the phone. "Hello."

"Hello. It's Brad. It's not like I'm just sitting around all day with nothing better to do than call you, but I do keep thinking about you. You have a pleasant telephone voice even if you don't use it much. I mean you're not real talky, you know?"

"Yes."

"Well, I figured it wouldn't hurt to call again. I mean I know you said not to, so I hope I'm not being offensive."

Silence.

"OK, I know you like to read. Can I ask what you're reading?"

"Why?"

"Because I'm just floundering around here trying to make conversation and that seemed like maybe a safe topic?"

"OK."

"Well, what are you reading?"

"*The Silent Patient*," by Michaelides."

"Michaelides? Never heard of him."

"Me neither. It's his first novel."

"Is it good? Do you like it?"

"That's two separate questions, isn't it?"

"I guess so, but you probably wouldn't like it if it wasn't good."

"You may be giving me too much credit."

"Credit?" he asked.

"For good taste I guess; assuming I wouldn't like it if it wasn't good."

Whatever Brad had, some combination of awkward charm, earnestness, and, of course, persistence, it was working. Alma was still on the phone and conversing, somewhat.

Brad asked her for a date.

"No."

"OK, well, how about if we just meet for coffee or a drink?"

"How would that be different from a date?"

"Umm, I don't know. Maybe you could pay for yours?"

"No."

"No, you won't pay or no you won't go?"

"The latter. No, both."

Brad laughed, "Man, you are tough. OK, I've tried. Can I call you again?"

"Didn't you ask that before, and I said No? And here you are anyway?"

"I guess that's right. OK. Well, surprisingly, I've enjoyed talking with you. Although it does feel kind of like a fencing match. Not that I've ever been in a fencing match. Figure of speech, you know?"

"OK. Bye."

Alma hung up. She briefly wondered why she'd stayed on the phone, but if you'd asked, she'd have denied being lonely or bored. The staying on the phone, and especially the wondering about why she did, was definitely a bit of introspection, and definitely unAlmish, not the same old Alma we've known and loved for so long.

But she wasn't surprised the next time that Brad called, nor any of the times after that.

Of course, one thing led to another, as one things so often do, and Brad was persistent without seeming pushy and then they were "dating," kind of, Alma still cautious. Then, kind of suddenly, they were living together, and being intimate, both in the sensual sense of the word and in the other sense, sharing their lives and the stories of their lives.

Brad of course shared more detail and more of his feelings than Alma. Alma generally didn't share feelings; she didn't like being that open, she wasn't very aware of what her feelings were, and, without her being conscious of it, she was afraid of finding out.

But she was a good listener, and she was intrigued by Brad's story.

BRAD'S STORY, AS TOLD TO ALMA

Brad and the orthopod were half brothers, not brothers. Their father was a general surgeon, known less for his skill than for his availability, that is, in his professional work, not to his sons, although the term `available' could also apply to him in other ways. He often took weekend and night call for other surgeons to rack up more money. So the family had a good life, financially.

Brad's half brother was the only child of the father's first marriage, to an airline stewardess who'd never wanted children. Two days after the boy's first birthday she ran off with a Puerto Rican airline pilot.

A year later the father married a lady realtor whose primary interest was her business. She also hadn't wanted children but after a night of partying she became pregnant with Brad. She was Brad's mother only in the biological sense. This may have been a good thing for Brad as while she was an excellent realtor she wasn't cut out to be a mother, which required a different skill set. Brad was three when she left the father after discovering he was dallying with not one, not two, but three different nurses, unbeknownst to each other of course. How he had time to do that as busy as he was cutting and sewing was a mystery to everyone.

The housekeeper, an illegal immigrant, resented the substitute mothering dumped on her as part of the job. She put up with it because she was afraid that she might get deported if she made any waves. She took it out on the boys. She finally got so fed up with the unfair burden and with the older boy's disrespect and unmanageable behavior that she took the risk and quit, having secretly found a much better job.

At the time, the older boy wasn't doing well at his expensive private school.

For example, when one of the younger teachers mildly chastised him for a small offense, the boy responded in Spanish, using words he'd learned from the immigrant maid, God only knows where she'd picked them up. The teacher could only respond with a bewildered look and order him to sit down, which he eventually did, after a few more Spanish words. The teacher didn't understand a thing he said, but another teacher happened to be in the classroom and also happened to be fluent in Spanish. She told the headmaster what she'd heard, although she chose not to translate all of the words.

Although the father always paid the exorbitant tuition promptly and occasionally hinted at a substantial donation to come at some unspecified future time, the school didn't appreciate the boy's cursing the teachers out in Spanish, nor his bringing marijuana to the school and sharing it with his friends and selling it to the others. Nor his obviously having his essays written by his younger brother, as he was too busy with more important matters to write them himself. So he'd been skating on thin ice for a while, in spite of his father's machinations. But then he hung the headmaster's tomcat from the flagpole, in such a skillful fashion I should add, being good with his hands already, that the poor animal wasn't harmed, unless cats can have post-traumatic stress disorder. In any event, the cat was never the same afterwards. The father preempted the boy's expulsion and sent him off to military school.

The brother had been spending time with Brad and had taught him how to read when he was five. He was the only attachment in Brad's life and his being sent away was a great loss.

At military school the older boy didn't do well scholastically, but he learned how to sail and how to ride a horse. During vacations, he taught these skills to Brad. Brad never cared for riding and actually was afraid of horses, but he took to sailing with enthusiasm, revealing a natural talent, and he soon became a better sailor than his older brother although the brother never acknowledged it. The boys continued riding and sailing together when they could into their adulthood.

The father never remarried after Brad's mother left. He'd learned about the harshness of alimony and he was able to get his needs met without the necessity of matrimony. He had a succession of live-in women friends in addition to housekeepers; few of them stayed around long.

One of the live-in friends, a childless widow, was the first woman in Brad's life to have any affection for him. A year after the immigrant housekeeper left, the father, over the widow's objections, sent eleven-year-old Brad to boarding school. He told the widow that he couldn't handle the responsibility of having a child in the house anymore, even though he'd never shown any inclination to handle it in the first place. The father was a workaholic and a prolific philanderer, so he'd never had time to be a father too. After Brad was sent off, the widow maintained some contact with him but only for a short while.

The father's sudden death came inopportunely; he dropped dead in the middle of an operation.

His usual nurse, their relationship mostly limited to work, was out with the flu. That was fortunate because the substitute assisting nurse was more competent. She staunched the blood flow and retrieved the dropped instruments from the abdominal cavity. She and the anesthesiologist kept the poor patient alive while the hospital administration scrounged up a surgical replacement. He finished the job and the patient fortunately survived, although with some brain damage due to the period of low blood pressure. While the nurse was performing her ministrations, the surgical tech was performing CPR on the father, futilely as the man had suffered a massive stroke and was instantly quite brain-dead.

After the blood was cleaned up, the dust settled, the ashes interred and the lawyers paid, the two ex-wives, the stewardess and the realtor, received lump sums.

Two of the long ago mentioned nurses, the dalliantes who'd prompted the exit of the second wife, threatened to cause trouble. It wasn't clear what kind of trouble they could legally cause but it was thought best to just pay them off.

After all these expenses, the boys received enough to sustain them in their further education.

The older boy was a college freshman and Brad a junior at the boarding school. They were shocked to learn of their father's untimely demise, but the news didn't unduly sadden them as they barely knew him.

And that was that.

Brad told Alma how his half brother had always been supportive of him, at least compared to their father, although they hadn't had much time together. Brad realized part of their connection was his brother's enjoyment of the role of the older brother, the teacher and superior, and Brad was careful not to make obvious that he was the better sailor. Thus the older brother preferred horseback riding together and Brad agreed to this because he treasured their time together even if it involved horses.

Brad idolized his brother and had wanted to become a doctor himself. Not a surgeon, but maybe a pediatrician, with more personal interaction, especially with the mothers. And he liked children. But in college he could make no sense of organic chemistry, even with the help of tutors, so he took it a second time. On his second try, he passed the first exam, barely. The second exam, he tripped up on the Krebs Cycle,

"The sequence of reactions by which most living cells generate energy during the process of aerobic respiration. It takes place in the mitochondria, consuming oxygen, producing carbon dioxide and water as waste products, and converting ADP to energy-rich AT."

Although he'd studied the Cycle intensively he'd never understood it, but he thought he had it memorized. Apparently not well enough. On the third question, he was required to list the steps of the Cycle:

Step 1: Citrate synthase...
Step 2: Aconitase. ...
Step 3: Isocitrate dehydrogenase. ...
Step 4: a-Ketoglutarate dehydrogenase. ...
Step 5: Succinyl-CoA synthetase. ...
Step 6: Succinate dehydrogenase. ...
Step 7: Fumarase. ...
Step 8: Malate dehydrogenase...

Can you believe he got steps four and five reversed and left out step seven entirely? Well, he did. If it'd been me, I'd have used a mnemonic, like "Can an isolated Kraut send several funny messages?" But who am I to comment? I myself didn't ace organic chemistry, not by a long shot. Fortunately, organic isn't included in my teaching load at the college.

Brad passed the course, barely, using tutors and a bit of cheating. His grades weren't going to get him into medical school, at least not in this country. And with a foreign degree he'd always feel second class, although his advisors said that was unrealistic. So Brad graduated with an engineering degree and a minor in business, with average grades.

Brad had attended an inexpensive state college, which also lessened his chances of getting into medical school, so he had money left over from his inheritance. With a small loan from his brother, which he later came to regret although he couldn't see any other option, he bought a medical supply business. He realized that the brother liked making the loan and wasn't disappointed that Brad didn't go to medical school. But Brad treasured what he thought was a bond between them and he tolerated his brother's superiority complex.

Brad had more talent for business than for chemistry and his compassion for patients and for their families helped his medical supply business thrive. Amazingly, he soon owned four medical supply stores in two different cities, all successful. He was good at choosing locations. It was satisfying to pay off the loan although it didn't please the brother.

Brad bought a medical bookstore near a large medical center. He had sympathy for the medical students, especially the poor ones, and he set up a system for trade-ins of the obscenely expensive medical textbooks, which the students rarely had time to read. But some of the students, the "gunners," a term of both admiration and derogation, actually read some of the texts, foregoing sleep and other normal human activities in striving to be at the top of their class. Unfortunately, this group had a higher suicide rate than the average medical student population.

Brad's book trade-in system worked well. Unlike college, where most of the professors, who we well know are not highly paid, wrote their own texts, made them required reading, and updated them often precisely to thwart the trade-in economy, the medical texts were generally high quality classics and stable in their requiredness.

Brad's brother introduced him to some of the doctors and professors in the medical center. Brad's personality and his interest in medicine attracted more of them. And he'd notify them when something of interest came in and he did special orders. Brad enjoyed his connections, his success, and his helping the students and trainees.

Brad became disenchanted with his brother's womanizing, his focus on accumulating wealth and his flaunting of it, such as his two top of the line Lexi, and his drinking, that is, his behavior while drinking. Although the brother continued to drink heavily and had no wish to moderate his intake, he faithfully attended AA meetings twice a week, as required by the medical board to keep his license after complaints from an operating room nurse. She'd reported him twice for performing surgery while intoxicated. Despite his impairment he'd done an adequate job. The patients happened to be male and hadn't suffered damage except for excessively prominent scars which the men, being men, weren't concerned about.

After the nurse reported him, she was of course promptly fired on trumped up grounds by the hospital, which made a profit on the doctor's surgeries. With the nursing shortage, she soon got another job with better pay, better benefits and better scheduling.

Brad's involvement with his brother lessened further after he moved in with Alma. Brad and Alma had quickly settled into a comfortable routine. They got along well.

Almost always.

Almost.

ALMAS'S LIFE WITH BRAD AND THE DEATH OF ALMA'S MOTHER

In the middle of their first December together, Brad and Alma repaired to the living room after dinner as usual. Brad asked, "Are we putting up a tree?"

"No."

Brad surveyed the sparsely furnished room. "Look, there's plenty of room. A tree would look nice in here." It wasn't that he'd always had a Christmas tree during his childhood; it was that he hadn't.

"No. No tree."

"OK," Brad said. "But here." He drew a small nicely wrapped package from his briefcase. "I was going to wait and put this under the tree, but I'll give it to you now. Merry Christmas."

He extended the package towards Alma, but she made no move to accept it.

"No, thank you. I don't do Christmas."

"You don't do Christmas? What do you mean?"

"What do you mean, what do I mean? I. Do. Not. Do. Christmas."

"Didn't you have Christmas when you were a kid?" Brad asked.

"Yes, more or less."

"Was it bad? Did something happen?"

"It wasn't good, it wasn't bad. You never knew. But there wasn't any great trauma, if that's what you're asking. I just don't do Christmas. Let's not talk about it anymore."

"OK. OK, I guess. But please, take the present."

Brad didn't notice that Alma's lips were set in a tight line.

"OK," Alma said, and took the package. She carefully unwrapped it, neatly folded the paper and set it and the ribbon on the sofa beside her as though she was going to save it, although the wrapping had a Christmas theme on it and she wasn't.

She slowly took the lid off the small box, wrestled with the white tissue papers, and extracted a small silver pin with a semi-precious stone just off center.

Brad didn't know Alma very well yet. She didn't do Christmas and she rarely wore jewelry.

Alma examined the pin and then placed it back in the box.

"It's very pretty," she said. "Thank you." She closed the lid, set the box down on top of the wrapping paper, and picked up the book she'd been reading.

"Aren't you going to put it on?" Brad asked.

Alma's lips grew even tighter. "Not now. Another time." She opened her book.

Brad had spent a lot of time selecting the pin. He'd gone to several jewelry stores searching for the right gift. When he found this pin, he thought it really suited Alma, with a clean simple style, and a small amethyst adding some color. He'd been excited about giving it to her. Brad's feelings were hurt, but Alma didn't notice.

Alma never wore the pin and Brad never asked her about it. He was getting to know her.

Her mother's death wasn't unexpected. It was either pretty fast or pretty slow, depending on your perspective and on when you started counting. She'd suffered abdominal pain for a year and seen three different doctors. The first diagnosed gall bladder disease and wanted to operate, but the ultrasound was normal. The second diagnosed diverticulitis. His antibiotics didn't help the pain but added diarrhea to her problems. The third was honest and said, "Beats the hell out of me," maybe not his exact wording. He referred her to G.I. and GYN specialists. After the month and a half wait for an appointment, the increasing severity of her pain and her sudden rapid weight loss tipped off the GYN. The tests showed ovarian cancer. Exploratory surgery revealed cancer all over the lining of her abdominal cavity and her liver. It may have been inoperable for quite a while.

She was referred to an oncologist for chemotherapy but she never made an appointment. She knew the drill. Three of her church friends had been through that ordeal and two had died anyway. The third was thriving, although she hadn't passed the five-year hurdle yet. She encouraged the mother to get treatment, but one out of three odds didn't appeal to Alma's mother. She didn't find her life that alluring anyway. She declined the benefit of further medical attention and resigned herself to dying, much to Alma's relief, although she'd carefully refrained from trying to influence her mother's decision.

Alma didn't spend much time with her mother but she did hire some caretakers. Some were good and some not so much. Eventually she found a hospice program, which was excellent. Alma's mother died peacefully at home eight months after finally getting her diagnosis and after one month of much less pain. Alma wasn't there when she passed but the hospice people did a superb job of taking care of everything.

Alma again made the funeral arrangements, which, unlike her father's, involved the church, and again, she paid for everything. She attended the service at Our Lady of Perpetual Something or Other, and this time she sat through it to the bitter end. The church was half full, which was pretty good considering that it was a large building with a congregation no longer commensurate with its size. Half the attendees were members who attended all the funerals but half were people who'd actually known Alma's mother and considered her a friend even though she wasn't a regular attendee.

Alma even went to the graveside service where a handful of those people showed up. While the priest droned on and on, Alma distracted herself by silently summarizing the last few books she'd read as though she were telling Brad about them. Then she remembered the last time she'd been intimate with Brad and the humorous comments he'd made in the midst of their lovemaking and she chortled to herself. This caused a few of the attendees to glance sidewise at her and the priest even paused in his droning and looked in her direction, so Alma faked a cough, stifled her amusement and shifted her mind back to literature.

After the service, she again shook hands with the attendees, fending off most of the hugs. Declining the funeral director's suggestion that she take some of the flower arrangements with her, she walked to her car, sat for a short time, and drove home. She poured herself a full glass of white wine, picked up a book on the settling of the West, frowning at the ethnocentric viewpoint, with frequent mentioning of "the savages." She read until she became sleepy. She went to bed with only two-thirds of her wine consumed and she slept well. Although she probably had dreams, she didn't remember any of them the next day.

And that was that.

Life of course went on. Alma enjoyed the library. She'd wander the stacks and pick five or six books to take to a table. She'd read a little in each one and check out the two that most caught her interest, leaving the rest for the librarians to shelve. She was a fast reader and had little else to do, so she was visiting the library twice a week or occasionally thrice. Her range of interests expanded. She liked fiction of several kinds - historical, mysteries that challenged the intellect, and family sagas. Romance, not so much. She was learning a lot from nonfiction, but also about human relationships and family dynamics from the fiction. She read a few books on those topics because she was getting a little curious about her own family.

Brad and Alma enjoyed discussing their reading. Brad liked current politics, Alma didn't, so they didn't discuss that. They both liked history although Brad didn't like historical fiction; he was a businessman and preferred facts. So Alma could read a historical novel and Brad the history of that period. Or one might recommend a book they'd liked and the other would read it. So they had plenty to discuss.

"I just finished this book," Alma said, "You might like it."

Brad looked up from his reading of an old medical text, *The Acute Abdomen* by Cope.

"What's it about?"

"It's about this woman in World War Two, very interesting, kind of a thriller."

"Well, that's not exactly my style, but would it have some history?"

"Sure, it does. It really held my attention. I think you'd like it."

"Okay, put it on my table, on the stack. I'll get to it pretty soon. This book, it's a surgery text, fascinating, first edition in 1926, about diagnosis, not cutting, and it's still up to date, even with all the new imaging and stuff. They still come in asking for it. It's in the twenty-second edition now. Quite a classic."

"That's nice, for a book to be good for so long, but it's nothing I'd ever want to read."

"No, of course not. I just admire it. The author's so clear and thorough in so few pages. Sometimes I wonder. What if I'd passed organic OK and got to be a doctor? Maybe a pediatrician, maybe a hospitalist with the really sick kids and the stressed out parents and some diagnostic questions. I think I'd have liked that."

Alma nodded. "I think you would've, too. You're always reading medical books. You'd have been good at it. You're kind and patient and good at explaining things, like you would to the kids, and the parents too. But I thought you were happy. I thought you were satisfied with what you're doing."

"I am. I am. No regrets. And I'm helping people and the business keeps me in medicine a little. No, I'm happy where I am. And I'm very happy with you."

"Umph," replied Alma, and picked up the next book on her stack, *Everyone Brave Is Forgiven,* by Cleave. The cover annoyed her; it had a small icon on it, "Instant New York Times Bestseller," and she couldn't tell if that referred to this book or to the author or what they meant by "Instant," but she thought it was overmarketing and confusing and she didn't like to be confused. She read the first page but she didn't give it a fair chance; she put it back on the stack and slid out the next book, *Smoke Screen,* by Mills.

"What's that one about?" Brad asked.

"Somebody at the library recommended it. It's something about the scandal with the cigarette companies." Alma's lips tightened, slightly annoyed because she was ready to stop talking and start reading. "Oh, that could be interesting," Brad commented. "medical and historical, too."

Alma didn't reply. She'd already finished the first page and was moving on. Brad took the hint and returned to his surgery book. Funny thing, later that month she picked up the Cleave novel again and liked it well enough. She even recommended it to Brad as showing a little known aspect of World War Two history.

Brad wasn't quite as good in bed as Anthony had been, being less experienced, but Alma tried not to compare them and she gave Brad no hint of her appraisal. But Brad was always considerate of her needs and she appreciated that, and she subtly taught him a few things without his realizing he was being taught. Some things she had no personal knowledge of, but her broad reading had yielded some interesting ideas. So their sex life was satisfying and kept improving.

Over time, Alma became more open about her childhood. Because Brad was sharing a lot and was a good listener, this was easier and more gratifying than she could've imagined. She hadn't gone into much detail about her siblings because there wasn't that much detail to share. But siblings still had some effect on her life, and soon that would also involve Brad.

ALMA'S VISIT WITH TWO

You remember Two, Alma's younger sister?

Two moved out of state as soon as she graduated from high school. She started working in a Dollar Store and eventually became the manager. Alma stopped sending the occasional small checks, but Two didn't mind and the sisters stayed in touch with occasional phone calls.

Two had hooked up with a guy who managed a mobile home sales lot. He didn't sound too bad to Alma, considering.

Shortly after their baby was born, Two asked Alma to come visit and meet her niece. Alma wasn't enthusiastic but Brad encouraged her to go. Since she'd never flown before, and in fact never would again, Brad said he'd travel with her and help with check-in and seat belting and all the rigamarole that was routine to those used to flying. After the flight landed, more bumpily than Alma appreciated, they rented a car and checked into a nice hotel not far from Two's trailer. Being near the coast, the nearby restaurants offered a range of fresh seafood, which delighted Brad. Alma still wasn't much interested in food.

The visit went OK. The boyfriend turned out to be OK. Two obviously appreciated Alma's coming, took her to the Dollar Store and introduced her around and told her to pick something, anything she wanted, on her. Alma picked up some knick-knack from China which she left in the trash at the airport on the return trip.

Alma was glad to see that the baby seemed healthy and anatomically intact. She encouraged Two to get the baby all of her shots. Two, slightly miffed, said she certainly intended to. They were both recalling the brother who'd died, although neither mentioned him. The trip lasted two days; Alma felt that was quite long enough. At the end, Two initiated a round of hugging, and then they repeated their goodbyes.

Two watched the car out of sight and then turned to her boyfriend and said, "Well?"

"Well, what? Did I do something wrong?"

"No, no, don't be so sensitive. What did you think of them?"

"Think of them?"

"Yeah, Dummy, what did you think of them? Of him? Of my sister?"

"Well, I liked him OK. I thought he was gonna be kind of a snob, but he was OK. They're rich aren't they?"

"I told you that. Yes, they're rich."

"Well, they didn't act like it, didn't show off and throw it around, but then they didn't spend much of it on us, did they?"

"I didn't want them to. That isn't why I asked her to come. And she helped me, showed me some things with the baby. So, what did you think of her?"

"Think of her?"

"Yeah, Dummy, that's what I'm asking you. What did you think of her?"

"I don't know. I didn't think of her that much. She seemed kind of stiff; is that what you mean?"

"Yeah, what else?"

"What else? Well, we didn't talk much, she never said much to me. She seemed interested in the baby, though. I guess she's alright, I got nothing against her."

"Well, good. She is my sister, she practically raised me, and she did come all the way out here when I asked her to, and she is the baby's aunt."

"That's right, she did. She is. She's OK. Hon, while you're up, could you get me another beer?"

And she did.

While this conversation was unfolding, Brad and Alma arrived at the airport. They were early for their flight and found a restaurant where Alma ate part of an indifferent salad while Brad savored one more lunch of fresh flounder, substituting onion rings for french fries at no extra charge.

On the flight back, Brad said that he'd liked Two and the boyfriend, who seemed nice enough and committed to Two and the baby, and was knowledgeable about cars and fishing, which is what he and Brad discussed over beers while Alma and Two visited and looked after the baby. Alma of course was quite experienced at this. She'd shown Two some useful tips and reassured her about a couple of concerns. Alma had seen a side of Brad that she hadn't known about and she was impressed that he could so easily get along with the boyfriend.

After Brad said he'd liked them, Alma said, "That's nice," and then they began talking about the new book they'd both read and they never mentioned the trip again.

In fact, Alma was a bit worried. She thought that Two was drinking too much and feared she might've been drinking while pregnant, although the baby looked alright. Two had offered them drinks as soon they arrived. They declined but Two consumed two large glasses of wine right away, and later that evening, two glasses of bourbon and coke, which Alma also declined but Brad and the boyfriend had beers. Alma hadn't mentioned any of these concerns to Two or to Brad. She told herself that Two was just tense about them being there, that's all, although she didn't really believe that. Alma was happy to be home again after the short flight.

And that was that, although Two and her child would come up again before long, and not in a good way.

ALMA'S LIFE WITH BRAD CONTINUES, FOR A TIME

In the evening Brad and Alma usually had soft music playing in the background, jazz or blues but never classical, which Brad would've enjoyed but Alma not. Alma usually had a glass of white wine, or half a glass, and Brad a scotch on the rocks, or rarely two; sometimes they had no alcohol at all. Neither had a drink unless they both did.

Alma didn't spend as much time with Brad as she had with Anthony. Brad was busy with his business during the day and didn't have the free time Anthony'd had, and he didn't have the wide range of interests that Anthony had exposed her to and he had no social engagements.

Brad occasionally stayed late at the bookstore or did some work at home in the room he used as an office, but usually he finished work by five and his business rarely ran into the weekend except during tax season. He was blessed with managers that he could rely on, not solely due to his being blessed but also because he was good at selecting them. Since most of them came from the sales ranks he knew them well before he promoted them, and, because he treated them well, the turnover rate of his employees was low.

Brad had one hobby, sailing. He owned a small sailboat. When he took Alma sailing for the first time, she got mosquito bites and a sunburn. She never went again but she was glad Brad could enjoy it. In good weather he went out for a day about once a month. He'd return home tired, hungry, and in good spirits. Alma would have prepared something for him to eat, something he'd enjoy but easy to make. After his sails, he always ate in the kitchen. Alma would sit with her wine while he ate and had a beer; he never drank his usual scotch after sailing, always beer. Alma asked him about this but he couldn't explain it.

"I don't know, it just seems like a beer goes with sailing somehow. Weird, isn't it?"

"Oh, I don't know. Whatever floats your boat, I guess." And they both laughed.

As Brad ate, he'd tell Alma about his voyage. He rarely discussed his work with her but he enjoyed talking about sailing. Alma liked listening and seeing his enthusiasm, and he appreciated her interest. He especially appreciated that she had no objections to his being gone for the day. He never considered that she might have reservations about his sailing and Alma tried to keep her anxiety to herself although her belief that sailing was dangerous was sometimes reinforced by the experiences he was sharing with her.

"I wish you could've seen this gorgeous sunset. It was spectacular this evening."

Or, " I saw the biggest seagull. I had some lunch left over so I threw him pieces to keep him around for a while. Then the joker came and grabbed a piece right out of my hand. Startled me. I ignored him after that and he finally left. Big sucker."

Things like that he'd share with her.

Occasionally Brad's trips were more exciting. Once he rescued a couple whose boat had capsized. They were both wearing life jackets and weren't in any danger but it took a lot of time and effort to get their boat righted again. They were fortunate that Brad was there because they didn't have the skill or the muscle to do it.

"Wasn't that dangerous?" Alma asked, unable to hide her nervousness.

"Nah," snorted Brad. "There's not much to it if you know how. You're supposed to practice it in your training, which apparently these guys never had. They really shouldn't rent boats to people unless they have some kind of training certificate."

"They were lucky you were there."

"I guess so," Brad replied, finishing off his beer and leaning back to drop the bottle in the trash can.

Another time Brad got caught in a storm. He never went out without checking the weather forecast, but this storm appeared unexpectedly and it gave him some trouble. In fact, he'd been a little scared, but he didn't share that with Alma. He told her how he'd handled the sails and it was obvious that he knew what he was doing. He rode the storm out, but he was late getting home, his meal was cold, and Alma had been worried.

"I'm glad you're home; I was getting nervous. What happened?"

"Well, there was a squall and I couldn't get back in `til it passed. Sorry you were worried."

"Couldn't you have called?"

"Yeah, I should've. I was late and wet and cold and I just wanted to get home and I just didn't think about calling. I'll call if I'm ever late like this again. I hope it won't happen though."

"We didn't have any storm here so I had no idea what was happening. Were you scared out there?"

"Of course not," Brad lied. "You know I'm a pretty good sailor. I just needed to wait it out. And I promise, I'll call if I'm going to be late again."

"OK. I'll heat up your dinner. You'll probably enjoy some hot food. It's spaghetti with your favorite sauce."

"Great! I think I'll skip the beer tonight. I'm gonna have me a scotch, straight up. Warms the blood."

Alma had nothing she considered a hobby, but she enjoyed the gym and walking, and most of all, reading.

And she enjoyed just being with Brad, which was reciprocal.

The tensions that had come between Alma and Anthony never developed with Brad. Brad's life didn't revolve around her like Anthony's had, although Brad cared for her at least as much. Brad appreciated her continued growing, but he wasn't invested in it. Alma appreciated both the caring and the independence; she now could have both a relationship and the independence that Mary Alma had vowed to attain so long ago.

Alma had less insecurity, with its wariness and need to maintain control. When she was a little controlling, Brad, who had more self-confidence and independence than Anthony, didn't find her very irritating, really, not irritating at all. "That's just Alma," he'd think and go on with whatever he was doing.

To summarize and tidy up, Brad and Alma settled into a comfortable routine and were satisfied with their relationship and their lives.

But the night of Brad's stormy sailing adventure, Alma had a nightmare. In her dream, her brother was lying in bed screaming for help and no one was around. Alma felt his forehead and he was burning with fever. Alma couldn't find her mother. She went to get the boy some water but when she turned the handle, nothing came from the faucet. She felt scared and helpless. When she went back to his bed it was empty. She screamed for her brother and then for her mother but there was no answer.

She woke with Brad shaking her gently. "Alma! Alma! Wake up!"

Alma turned to him. "What?"

"You were screaming. You had a bad dream. Are you OK?"

"Yeah, I'm OK. Sorry I woke you."

"That's OK. I'm sorry you had a nightmare; it must've been awful. What was it about?"

"I don't remember," Alma lied. She didn't want to get into it, and she only vaguely remembered that it was about her brother and had been filled with an awful feeling of lack of control. "Let's go back to sleep."

Alma rolled over but she couldn't get back to sleep right away. She was thinking about her brother and then she started thinking of her sisters. "Oh well, that's all over and it was a long time ago," she said to herself. "Nothing I can do about it. It's stupid to even think about it." She started thinking about the novel she was in the middle of. She liked it although she thought the female protagonist was over-reactive and might feed the stereotype of a hysterical female. Alma started playing in her mind with different ways the novel might turn out and soon fell asleep.

The next morning Brad asked her about the nightmare. She could truthfully tell him that all she remembered was he woke her up in the middle of the night, but she didn't hold it against him.

Brad, whose therapy had been helpful, was a little more introspective than Alma. Hell, everyone was a little more introspective than Alma. Brad occasionally made efforts to get closer, or to get her to open up a bit, or to be a little more self-aware. Once he even suggested she might benefit from therapy.

"Therapy? Why in the world would I want therapy?"

"Well, it's been useful to me, and it might be helpful to you."

"Helpful how, may I ask?" Alma was too sophisticated and well-read to say, "I don't need therapy; I'm not crazy," or as Barbara Bush commented when discussing her problems with depression, "I didn't need therapy; I'm not looney-tunes."

Brad responded carefully, "Therapy could help you be more comfortable, and you might understand yourself better. You had a rough childhood, and maybe you could resolve some issues."

"Issues? What do you mean, issues?"

"Well, you know, about your father and the violence, and your mother, and her drinking and not being there for you. Those things."

Alma's lips tightened. "My childhood wasn't any worse than yours, and that was a long time ago. I can't change anything about it now; it was what it was. Listen, I've read Freud and some therapy stuff and I don't see any point in digging around and stirring up old muck. It's a lot of self-pity and a waste of time. I run my own life, thank you, and I'm not gonna pay somebody to sit and listen to me blaming my parents for my problems that I don't think I have anyway. And just what makes you think I'm uncomfortable?"

Brad thought this was quite a long speech for Alma and that she was showing more passion than usual. He thought he needed to back off and fast.

"OK, OK, I think you're fine just the way you are; I'm not trying to get you to change. I'm just a big fan of therapy and I think almost anyone could benefit from it. I get too enthusiastic about it sometimes. I don't think you're gonna go to therapy, and that's fine. That's fine; I like you just the way you are."

"Humph," replied Alma, and picked up the book she'd been reading.

And that was that.

Brad never mentioned therapy again; well, he still talked about his own therapy occasionally, but never in any way suggesting that it for Alma. That was wise of him, don't you think?

The book Alma had been reading during the therapy discussion, or argument, or whatever it was, was *Sapiens,* by Harari, an Israeli historian. Brad had recommended it to her and she was enjoying it. Actually, she'd enjoyed the first third, about ancient humans, but she thought the middle third draggy. But she'd trudged through that and was enjoying the last part. They were discussing the book after dinner.

Alma mused, "That was interesting about happiness. Once you achieve some level of subsistence, more money doesn't make you happier, at least not after a brief time. As your income goes up, so do your expectations. Interesting idea."

Brad, of course, was interested in Alma.

"Well," he asked, "What's been your experience? You've been poor and now you're not. What do you think?"

"Yeah, after I made some money I was happy. But more money made me more comfortable. The more I had, the more I was sure I'd never have to depend on anybody. That didn't make me happier, but it made me more comfortable. I don't think that's the same thing. But maybe it is."

"Yeah, you've said independence is important, that you weren't gonna get trapped like your mother."

Alma didn't appreciate the reference to her mother. She rarely thought of her mother and she preferred it that way. "Right. I'm my own woman. Anyway, I've almost finished this book. Let me see how it ends." And she picked up her wine glass and returned to the book, which was fairly thick.

Brad started to say that they could talk about this again when she'd finished the book and that finishing that book was an accomplishment, but he noticed that thin set of the mouth and he let it drop. He guessed the conversation was getting too personal for Alma. He felt sad about that, but he realized how much more open she'd become since they'd met.

Alma had picked up the big book, but she wasn't reading yet. She'd had an unpleasant feeling that had been coming more often lately. She told herself, "I am happy. And comfortable. So why does it feel like something's missing? I'm with Brad. I've got money. I'm learning a lot. I've come so far. So what is this?"

Alma appreciated the knowledge she'd gained, the broadening of her interests, and her enjoyment of things she'd never imagined being involved in. Brad recognized her emotional growth but if he, or you, had mentioned that to Alma she wouldn't have known what you were talking about, and she would've quickly denied it, as though she was being accused of something bad. Yet her ability to notice these feelings of something missing and to wonder about them was introspection, wasn't it? New territory for Alma.

"What could be missing? Nothing's missing. Stupid. Forget it." Alma didn't notice that she'd said this out loud, but either Brad didn't hear her or he thought it best to let it go.

Alma resumed reading. She'd had these feelings and thoughts before. She didn't like them and she knew how to escape them.

INTERLUDE

At this point in the story my wife stared off into space for a minute. Then she surveyed the room. "I don't see her now," she said, "Maybe she's already left. She never was much for socializing; I wonder why she even came. I don't think she has any connection with the college."

My wife waved her empty glass at me. "Anyway, that's all I know about Alma and I'm thirsty. Go get me another Pinot, please."

"That would be your second," I reminded her.

"Now don't you start counting," she said, "and don't wander around trying to find Alma or get yourself taken up by that bar girl."

"Well, of course not," I replied.

But although I did look for Alma I didn't see her and when I got to the bar the girl was busy and didn't recognize me from before. Even so I left her another nice tip, guessing she might be working her way through college. I got the Pinot and another beer and went back to where my thirsty wife was waiting.

I was still interested in Alma. "So, she's rich, is she?"

"Rich? I guess you could say so. Yeah, you could. Richer'n both of us put together."

"How do you know all this stuff about her? You've told me a lot."

"Well, I've hardly ever spent any time with her; she pretty much sticks to herself. But she's family. I mean she was married to Ed. You know how families talk. Especially if someone is different. So she gets lots of talk."

"Umm. I see what you mean. How's the wine?"

We left the party soon after that, didn't even finish our drinks, and I never saw Alma again. I didn't think about her and never heard any more about her until many years later, after my dear wife was gone. Breast cancer, horrible, and I miss her every day. But also I was pissed that she hadn't waited and let me go first like I'd hoped. Still, I had my teaching and my life, dull though they were, and I kept trudging dutifully on through the slowly unfolding years. I was unprepared when the topic of Alma came up again.

I was standing at a bar drinking blended scotch, thinking maybe I'd been doing a little too much of that lately. I was mostly drinking at home, alone. Very alone. But I was at the bar drinking and talking with an old friend I hadn't seen for a while and we started talking about a book we'd both read, *The Boys in the Boat*. We'd both liked it a lot.

"That reminds me," he said. "You remember Alma?"

I couldn't recall any "Alma" for a minute; these days there's a lot of things I don't recall for a minute but they usually come back to me. And as I said, I hadn't thought about Alma for years. But then it clicked.

"Oh, yeah, I guess so," I said. "I never really knew her, never met her personally, but I know who she is."

"Was," he corrected me. He took a long swig of his drink. "Was. She passed a few months ago. What reminded me was she's the one that recommended the book to me, good choice. She was really something, sharp as a tack, richer'n God, and working at the library right up to the end. I kinda got to know her cause I hang out at the library a lot, you know, and sometimes when it was slow there we'd get to talking, you know. I think she was kind of lonely, maybe. She sure knew her books."

He finished his drink in one gulp, waved to the bartender for a refill but just for himself, didn't offer to get me one, and started telling me what he knew about Alma.

ALMA AND BRAD AND AFTER

Alma thought her life with Brad was nearly perfect. She hesitated to say "perfect," but she couldn't think of anything she'd want to be different. Still, some cynic said that nothing good ever lasts.

Alma wasn't disturbed by the changes of age. She kept up her appearance and was pleased that her face and body didn't age as fast as many other women's. Alma wasn't vain but since her dress shop days when appearance was critical, she'd believed that everyone should try to look their best. She wasn't upset when she finally needed glasses and she enjoyed picking out attractive frames so much that she bought several pairs so she could color coordinate. And also in case she lost a pair, because she noticed that she was starting to misplace things occasionally. She reduced her gym sessions from four a week to three and her workouts were shorter and less intense. She didn't walk as often nor as far and she usually carried a book with her because she was spending more time in the coffee shop where she'd read and chat with Arnid, who was no longer a young woman. She'd bought out her partners and was now the full owner of the shop. She reminded Alma of her younger self.

Other times Alma would drop into the library and check on the new acquisitions or chat with a familiar patron before resuming her walk.

Alma continued to read voraciously but she noticed that she didn't retain information as well and she occasionally had to re-

read passages to get their meaning. She expanded her range of reading, searching for topics she hadn't previously explored. She continued to enjoy fiction, but she was pickier, "Life is short and there's no reason to spend time on mediocre novels." Then she'd add, "Nor on drinking bad wine."

Alma read a lot about Buddhism but she never became a Buddhist. Meditation wasn't for her, but she tried to practice "just being," which she never could find a satisfactory definition for but was satisfying anyway. And she tried to eliminate striving from her life, to be satisfied with herself and her life as they were, although striving had never been a big factor in her life. She thought it amusing that she was striving to reduce striving.

Like everyone above a certain age, Alma had some concern about Alzheimer's, but she'd read enough to realize that the changes she noticed, the memory changes and the slow retrieval of words, especially names, were normal aging. And she was reassured that as far as she knew, there was no Alzheimer's in her family and that people who were concerned about Alzheimer's were rarely the people who actually had it. Those people usually were either unaware or in denial. She ignored the fact that she knew little about her grandparents or any other family; they could've all had Alzheimer's or anything else and she wouldn't have known.

She was pleased that while Brad showed physical signs of aging, he didn't show any of the mental changes she was observing in herself.

Alma accepted herself as she was without much self-reflection or attention to her feelings. However, in spite of what she'd said to Brad, she'd enjoyed a couple of books about psychotherapy although not drawn to indulge in it. She actually had a brief period of reflecting on her childhood and how it might have affected her. She knew she'd never forgiven her father, and she wasn't aware of any need to forgive her mother, who had just been her mother. She wondered about her grandparents and the close-mouthed secrecy in her family, but she didn't see any of that affecting her now and it didn't seem important. She soon ended this reviewing of the past. She thought, "OK, it was what it was and it's stupid to waste time and energy on what you can't do anything about."

This attitude was labeled in the therapy books as denial, suppression, and so forth, and unhealthy. But in some it was accepted as reasonable as long as the person was functioning well, which Alma thought she certainly was and which no one could find much evidence to refute. Certainly not Brad, who was happy with Alma just as she was, which is one of the bases for a strong satisfying relationship and also is relatively rare.

Brad had benefitted from several years of therapy with two different therapists, both women. Now he occasionally saw a therapist for one or two sessions, "a tune-up." This man, a few years younger than Brad, had a different approach. He'd listen intently to Brad for a few minutes and then start lecturing and advising. Brad learned to quickly list the issues he wanted addressed while he still had a chance to talk, rather than ventilating and rambling wherever he wished as in his previous therapies.

When he discussed his sessions with Alma, she said this sounded unlike any therapy she'd read about, but Brad said it was surprisingly helpful although he'd had doubts at the beginning. And if he did need to ventilate, Alma was ready to listen and was supportive and nonjudgmental, rare traits, hard to find outside of therapy.

It shows how well Alma and Brad were getting along that she made no critical or sarcastic comments about his therapy, although such comments may have entered her mind.

Alma was no longer her old wary self, so when the bottom dropped out from under her, she was totally unprepared.

After a light dinner of a delicious salad with a special avocado dressing, one of Brad's favorites, Alma and Brad were sitting in the living room listening to Dave Brubeck, I think. Alma was halfway through a novel, *The Guestbook.* I don't recall what Brad was reading. Alma had barely begun sipping her white wine.

She looked up at Brad. "You know, I don't really like this book. There's too many characters and it jumps around and I can't keep straight who's who. It's confusing. And I don't like the author's style. He tries too hard to be artsy. Listen, `This soft gray evening like lambswool -.' It's too, I don't know, too cute?"

"Then why are you still reading it? Life's too short and there's too many good books to be reading something you don't like."

Alma would find herself replaying that statement over and over in the next few months.

"Well, there's kind of a plot, more like five plots, and it has me hooked. I want to know how it turns out."

"Well, I hope you enjoy it. As for me, I believe I'll take this golden opportunity to go to the bathroom. Excuse me, please."

"You are excused. Hurry back."

Brad laid his book face down on the sofa, which slightly annoyed Alma, but not enough to comment on it yet again. It was his habit.

Brad stood up, yawned, stretched, made a grunting sound, "Unngh," and crashed to the floor. He hit his head hard as he landed.

"Brad!"

Brad made no response.

Alma jumped up, dropping her book on the floor and knocking her wineglass over, and rushed to his side.

"Brad!"

No response.

"Brad!"

Alma shook him and he still didn't respond. Even with all her reading, of so many topics, Alma knew nothing about first aid and she had no idea what she should do.

When Brad stretched, he'd dislodged part of a clot that had been lurking silently in his left carotid artery for years, and now traveled up to his brain, creating a massive stroke. Or maybe the stretch had nothing to do with it; maybe it was just time for the clot to break loose. You never can tell.

Alma rushed to her purse, found her phone, and called 911. Brad began having a seizure.

It seemed like a lot of rings before there was an answer. She was standing by Brad and shifting from foot to foot. "C'mon. C'mon!"

"What is your emergency, please?" The lady sounded pleasant and calm, maybe too calm to suit Alma.

"My husband! He fell and now he's having a seizure and he won't answer me. Please send an ambulance. Quick!"

Technically, Brad wasn't Alma's husband; he would've been her common-law husband in fifteen other states and the District of Columbia, but that's totally irrelevant right now.

"Is he breathing?"

"Yes, yes. He's breathing, kind of gasping. He's having a seizure. Please send someone now!"

"Is this your address?" The operator read the address on her screen because of its connection with the telephone number. Amazing modern technology.

"Yes. Yes! Please send somebody. The seizure stopped. He's just lying there. Brad! Brad! He won't answer me."

"Ambulance is on the way. Does your husband have any heart trouble? Has he ever had a seizure before?

"No. No. Tell them to hurry."

I don't want to put a lot more exclamation points in here but you get the idea.

"They're on the way. Should be there in a couple of minutes. Stay calm."

"What do I do? How can I help him?"

"No, no, you're doing fine. Just stay calm. They'll be right there. Is he still breathing?"

"Yes. That awful gasping."

"OK. The ambulance crew's hearing our conversation and they'll be there in a minute. Just stay calm."

"I am calm, dammit! Could you please quit telling me to stay calm?"

"Yes, I'm sorry. Just stay calm. They say for you to unbutton his shirt."

"OK. OK, just a minute."

This request might save a few precious seconds when the ambulance crew arrived but more likely it was just to give Alma something to do so she wouldn't feel so helpless and frantic. A good move.

Brad lay on his left side, still gasping. His buttons were difficult to undo, especially because Alma was in such a rush. As she finished the last button she heard the siren. She ran to open the door and two emergency techs rushed in with their equipment. They asked Alma what had happened, but they were already starting an IV and placing pads on Brad's chest for EKG monitoring.

"I don't know. He stood up and then he fell. He crashed. I think he hit his head. And he wouldn't answer. And then he started jerking. And there wasn't anything I could do and I just called."

"You did fine lady; you did fine. His heart looks good. Looks like he's had a stroke. He has a face droop. We're taking him in. Can you follow us?"

"No. I mean yes. Where are my car keys? Can't I just ride with you?"

"No, ma'am. Against the rules. You just park in the emergency lot and come on in to the desk. It'll be fine. Don't worry now."

Don't worry. Hah!

Meanwhile, a third EMT had rolled a stretcher in and the first two lifted Brad onto it while he held the IV bag up high. They strapped on an oxygen mask and rolled him into the ambulance and shut the doors, more or less in Alma's face while she stood momentarily paralyzed. They took off, fast, siren blaring, and Alma snapped to and ran to find her keys.

Brad, like his father before him, had suffered a massive stroke, but unlike his father, Brad didn't die immediately. He lingered in the hospital for three days, unable to speak, but communicating with Alma with head shakes, nods, and hand squeezes. Alma never left the hospital, although she didn't spend all the time at Brad's side. She took frequent breaks, getting books from the hospital library and reading them in the cafeteria, where the food wasn't as bad as you might expect, which mattered not at all to Alma.

Alma read several books while Brad was in the hospital, but afterwards she couldn't recall any of them. Still, they helped her get through the ordeal, not from their content, they weren't that kind of books, which are rarely helpful anyway, but just by having something to read. Reading had always been one of her most effective coping mechanisms.

On his third day in the hospital, Brad suffered a new bleed into the area of his original stroke. He became unresponsive, but Alma continued to spend time by his bed, holding the hand not tied down for the IV. He died that night. Alma was in the cafeteria reading about Mary, Queen of Scots, but she looked up when one of Brad's nurses came in, looked around, and headed for her with an expressionless face and Alma knew right away.

Brad's funeral, like her father's, was at the funeral home and brief. The funeral director spoke a few words about Brad and his life that Alma had written out for him, and he inserted a few words about Alma that she hadn't given him and didn't appreciate.

Alma was surprised by the number of people who turned up, none of whom she knew personally nor cared to, but she endured words of condolence, handshakes, and the occasional hug without flinching or grimacing. She didn't, however, go to the graveside, then or ever. Alma didn't care for funerals but she thought they were not only expected but probably served some useful function which had been referenced if not clearly explained in a book she'd read. Yet this was her third one, and she couldn't see that she'd received any benefit from them.

By the way, it was obvious that Brad's brother hadn't come to the funeral although Alma had asked an ICU nurse to call him about Brad's stroke and then asked the funeral home secretary to call him about the death and later the funeral arrangements. Alma had no intention of speaking with him herself. It did look strange that he never showed up at the hospital either, especially with his being a doctor.

Alma was just as glad. Maybe his absence was related to his drinking, which had gotten heavier over the years, so heavy that he'd lost all his hospital privileges, although not his license, so he was still doing some kind of medical work, I have no idea what. Anyway, Alma never heard from him and there was no evidence that he knew or cared about Brad's death. You'll never read another word about him here, and I don't know about you, but frankly, I'm just as glad. OK, some you might have a morbid curiosity about the course of his life, downhill presumably, although miracles sometimes happen, but not often, and anyway, we're not going there, so you'll need to just suck it up and let's get on with our story.

After the funeral, Alma went home and poured a full glass of wine. She picked up the book she'd been in the middle of when Brad had his stroke. She didn't drink any of the wine nor read any of the book, just sat on the sofa with them until she got sleepy and then she went to bed. She slept soundly and the next morning she didn't recall any dreams. She got up at her usual time, poured out the warm wine, put the book in the bookshelf, showered and dressed. She skipped breakfast and went to the library where she wandered around without much purpose and unable to focus on anything. She went home and did some unnecessary cleaning. She skipped lunch. She ate a light early dinner and went right to bed. The next morning, she felt like her old self and slipped back into her regular routine.

And that was that.

Well, almost.

Two days after Brad's death the maid came as scheduled. Alma told her what had happened and the maid said, "Oh, my. I'm so sorry. He was a nice man."

"Yes. Yes, he was." Alma was startled to see tears in the maid's eyes. "Now, I'd like you to skip the apartment today and just pack up Brad's things. There's some boxes in the storage room. I'll give you an extra fifty dollars if you'll take it all to Goodwill; I know that's not part of your regular job."

"Yes, ma'am. But you don't need to pay extra. I'll be happy to do it for you and for Brad. This is a hard time for you and he was such a nice man."

"No, if you're doing something extra you deserve to be paid for it. Now don't argue about it. Just get everything packed up."

While the maid was bustling about with an arm full of Brad's clothes, Alma noticed one of the sweaters. It was a pleasant light brown, with some darker brown shades mixed in. Alma thought it was attractive.

"Hold on a minute. Let me look at that." She picked out the sweater. "I think I'll keep this one."

After the maid moved on, Alma held the sweater to her face. It did smell faintly of Brad. She hung the sweater in her closet and went back to reading. Several months later, she was getting ready for bed and the bedroom was chilly. She thought of the sweater. She put it on, but when she lay down the buttons were too large and she was uncomfortable. She tossed the sweater towards the closet and in the morning she hung it on the back of the bedroom chair. On the maid's next day, Alma handed her the sweater.

"Why don't you just keep it if you like or maybe you have somebody to give it to. There's no point in making a trip to Goodwill just for one sweater."

And so it was gone.

And I guess that was that.

ALMA'S SECOND CRUISE, NORMANDY

Alma resumed her usual routine, as much as possible without Brad, but she felt restless. Somedays she felt like she was just going through the motions. And things didn't have the same interest as before. She thought, "Maybe it's because I don't have anybody to share with. No, `cause that was never a problem before Brad and I didn't share everything with him anyway. I mean, I wasn't dependent on him. But I do miss him."

She had an unusually vivid dream and she remembered it the next morning. In her dream, Brad said, "Alma, you need to get moving." He'd paused, looked at her kindly, and repeated, "Get moving."

Alma was impressed with how vivid the dream had been and how clearly she remembered it, but she didn't believe in the significance of dreams, no matter what Freud said, and she quickly dismissed it.

But then she contracted for a new roof and a new paint job and she booked another cruise, mainly to escape while the house was being worked on. Her other reason for the cruise was that she didn't know what else to do.

She used the same cruise line as before. For a small additional fee, she reserved a solo table, but still, on two occasions early in the voyage she was approached at dinner by gentlemen who asked if they could join her. At least the first had been a gentleman. She rebuffed him without being rude or crude but firmly, and loudly enough so that the other diners could hear. The second must not have heard her rebuff the first. And he seemed deficient in the visual department as well, poor fellow.

"Say, beautiful lady, couldn't help but notice you from all the way 'cross the room, and you look kind of lonely. I'll join you and we can have a pleasant dinner and it'll sure be pleasant for me while I'm looking at you."

Alma frowned. "If you thought I look lonely you might want to have your eyes tested, especially if you couldn't see that this table has only one chair, as I requested so I wouldn't be bothered, if you get my meaning."

Alma glared at the man, who was still standing there. He hadn't taken the hint, if you could call it that. She sized him up. He was nice looking but overweight, with a bit too much hair, and his hairdo a bit too fancy, and the handkerchief sticking out of his jacket pocket was off turning. She thought, "Maybe he's a little drunk, or maybe just a jerk. Or both. Or maybe a predator, looking for lonely women. Well, that's not me." She felt that she needed to protect herself, but she was more aware of feeling annoyed. Whatever he was, and she'd never know for sure, it really didn't matter. No matter who or what he was, Alma didn't want his company, nor anyone else's, especially male. The man apparently didn't appreciate her response to his charming approach.

"Well! Excuuuse me!"

"You are indeed excused. Do I need to call the waiter to guide you away or can you see well enough to move along? Now."

"Well, gee, you don't have to be that way about it." He still hadn't moved.

"Apparently I do. Waiter! Waiter, could you show this gentleman to a more appropriate table? At once, please."

The waiter, who was clearly sharper than the aforementioned gentleman, immediately grasped the situation and also grasped the man's upper arm. His captive was propelled several yards off before he could say anything or jerk away. Then the propellee said something under his breath which Alma didn't quite catch nor care to but which seemed to motivate the waiter to propel him even faster and with a firmer grip, causing the gentleman to speak more clearly, "Ow, dammit!" Alma heard that clearly. It caused a small smile.

Other passengers witnessed this skit and it was talked about around the ship for a day until something else interesting to gossip about came up. Alma wasn't bothered again for the rest of the cruise and she ate and read in peace. The service was excellent which she appreciated and the food was good which didn't matter to her as long as it wasn't bad. She sought the waiter out near the end of the trip and gave him a generous tip.

"Thank you, Sir Knight, for rescuing me from the dragon."

"And thank you, M'lady, you are most welcome. I must say it was a pleasure."

"Well, if I ever need a bodyguard."

"I shall be at your service, Madam."

Alma had chosen the Normandy cruise, featuring tours of the World War II beachhead and cemetery and lectures about D-Day, none of which she attended. She had an idea that her father had been in the D-Day invasion. He would never talk about the war so she had no data except her memory of the photo of the men with the rifles.

She was reading a book about D-Day from the ship's library when they docked in Normandy. She was disappointed that she couldn't see the famous beaches from the deck but she wasn't interested in a tour. She was close enough to the scene to satisfy the urge that had led her to choose this cruise. Alma stood by the rail and watched the tourists load into small boats. She stayed on the deck where it was quiet and pleasant and read her book:

"They were in the first wave. The soldier crouched low in the landing craft with his buddies. He tried to stay clear of the vomit in the bottom of the craft which was also occasionally flying through the air but it was impossible to evade. Everyone was crouched low except for the sergeant, who he didn't like but respected for his experience, and the sailor coxswain who was steering. The sergeant was standing so that he could see what was happening. What he saw was that as each landing craft grounded, about forty yards from the beach, as soon as the front ramp was lowered machine guns were firing straight into the open craft.

The sergeant started yelling. In the awful din of the guns from the ships and the shore, the soldier couldn't make out a word but he saw the soldiers near the sergeant start scrambling over the side of the landing craft.

Too much was happening all at once; the landing craft grounded, the coxswain dropped for shelter below the gunnel of the craft and the sergeant took three bullets in the head and one through his neck. The soldier scrambled over the side, too.

He was in trouble right away, loaded with a heavy pack and his rifle and in water over his head. He lost the rifle, which wasn't an important issue at that moment; his main concern was to avoid drowning. He hadn't come all the way over here just to drown. He managed to dog paddle until his toes could touch the bottom and he could shrug off his pack. Grabbing a body floating by, he pushed it ahead of him to protect himself from the bullets making little splashes in the water all around him. He noticed that some of the water was blue, some a dirty brown, and a lot of it red, and he thought it odd that he'd be paying any attention to the color of the water at this time.

He managed to get to the beach where he pushed the body aside and crawled to a small ridge of sand five yards up the beach, a very small ridge. When he reached it, he lay as flat as he could, trying to catch his breath and his thoughts. He was getting showered with sand as bullets hit the top of his ridge. After a short rest, he crawled on his belly over to a body lying nearby on his right to retrieve the rifle next to it. Then he saw that the rifle was shattered and the body was missing an arm. He paused for a moment, then rolled himself over the body and a few more yards to the next body. He was thinking that somehow rolling might be safer than crawling although when he replayed everything in his mind later, he realized that this made no sense.

He grabbed the rifle from the second body, still keeping flat. He was checking the weapon to see if it functioned and was startled when the body moaned. He reached for his first aid kit to get the morphine syrette but remembered that the kit had been strapped to his pack which was in the ocean. But it didn't matter; a mortar shell exploded just on the other side of the body and if he hadn't been lying right next to it, the shell would have gotten him, too. The syrette was no longer needed.

Lying there behind another very, very small sand dune, he wriggled and squirmed and tried to get lower, deeper into the sand, but it was wet and pretty firm. The occasional bullet, although he wouldn't have called them occasional, was hitting near the top of his dune and showering him with more sand.

Still lying flat, he raised the rifle, but not his head, and fired a round towards the front. He didn't expect to hit anything but he was relieved to see that the rifle worked. And he was grateful that the din had diminished, not realizing that he'd been partially deafened by the nearby explosion. He guessed that now he was ready for D-Day but he had no idea what the hell he was supposed to do next."

Alma closed the book and laid it on a nearby lounge chair. One of the stewards could pick it up later. She'd read all the D-Day she wanted to, ever. She was feeling slightly nauseous.

Alma stood at the rail for a long time. She skipped lunch. That evening she watched the tourists returning. They were not in their usual jovial mood. A few were softly talking among themselves but most were silent.

On the return trip, like on the trip over, Alma did nothing but read, but no more about the war, and watch the ocean. She thought the trip had been a good idea.

And then she was back home and at loose ends again, or she would've been, but there was a surprise waiting for her.

YET ANOTHER INTERLUDE

"Hold on," my friend said, leaning back from the bar and surveying the room. "Just a minute, all this talking about a cruise is making me thirsty, you know? Where the hell is that damn bartender when you need him?"

While we waited for the bartender, I guess he'd had to go to the john or something, or maybe he was closing a drug deal out in the parking lot, who knows, we both sat in silence, looking into our glasses, his empty and mine nearly so. I didn't know what to say. I hadn't known Alma, and I wondered why this story had such an impact on me. I realized that it was stirring up memories of my wife, of that terrible period at the end, although there were a few moments of sweetness there, too, but my reaction was more about Alma.

My friend interrupted my reverie, or train of thought, or whatever it was, when the bartender finally reappeared. My friend got his attention," Hey, Bud. Buddy!" and ordered a refill, again just for himself, but I had the presence of mind to indicate my glass and say, "Me, too."

"Umm," I finally said. "That's some story. She must've been quite a gal, but she really was kind of strange, wasn't she?"

"Guess so," he said, and swirled his drink before he took a sip. "Anyway, -" and he changed the subject.

"Whoa, whoa," I exclaimed. "I thought you were going to finish telling me about Alma."

"Oh, yeah. That's right. Guess you want the ending. I was afraid you might be getting bored with this or something, you know?"

"No, no. I'm interested. Don't leave me hanging."

"OK, if you're sure. Actually, I was afraid the ending might be upsetting to you, with your loss and all."

"Yeah, there's that. But I'm a big boy. Go ahead with the rest."

"OK then. Well,—"

ALMA'S IN BUSINESS AGAIN

When she got home from her cruise Alma would've been at loose ends again except for the three telegrams awaiting her from an attorney stating that she needed to contact him ASAP about Brad's will. Alma had no idea that Brad had a will. He'd never mentioned it to her.

Alma and Brad had never married. Brad had suggested the idea a couple of times but they'd agreed that it wasn't necessary. They considered themselves husband and wife, and they'd seen too many couples who'd lived together happily for years until they married and then became unhappy and then divorced, often bitterly.

"Why risk spoiling a good thing?" was Alma's view. Brad had never pushed it and the idea was dropped. They were happy as they were. Since they weren't married, things could've been messy after Brad's death, but he'd had the foresight and consideration to make a will. This made the legal process simpler and maybe less expensive, maybe.

Alma was the heir of Brad's estate. The cash portion was significant even after funds were distributed as stipulated and paying the lawyers who indicated that the situation was complicated and had required extra billable hours on their part (although of course most of the work had been done by their legal assistants).

Alma also inherited three medical supply stores and the medical bookstore. Brad had great faith in the staff of his first supply store. He left the manager the majority ownership and the rest of the shares to the other employees, according to how long they'd worked there. So Alma didn't get that store; the three other stores, along with the bookstore, were more than enough, thank you very much.

Alma put the cash in the bank. She'd decide what to do with it later, maybe give it to the library. The stores, however, needed attention and decisions now. She'd gone through this before, with the dress shops, but Brad's businesses were legitimate, so it was simpler.

Alma was no longer interested in owning stores. She arranged to meet the managers with her accountant. She spent a day at each store, interviewing the manager and employees, going over the books with the accountant, and observing the business operating.

She was impressed with the managers of two of the stores and the bookstore. Her lawyer arranged deals so they could purchase the stores on an installment plan, giving them favorable prices. Her accountant questioned her generosity but she straightened him out. She was no longer interested in being the sharp trader, the astute business person she'd once been.

Alma didn't think the third supply store was well-run. Some of the employees weren't well-dressed and the store wasn't as clean as it should be. One of the salespeople was chewing gum. Some of the bills for supplies were overdue. Alma was not impressed. She didn't fire anybody, although she did tell the one salesperson, rather sharply, to park the gum. But she put that store up for sale at a favorable price and it was quickly taken over by a chain.

Dealing with the stores took five weeks, from when she made the first visit to the last signing of papers. Although business was her forte, Alma didn't enjoy this task. She wasn't interested in this kind of thing anymore and since Brad's death she didn't have the energy or enthusiasm she'd had before. But she felt it was her responsibility to Brad, and to his employees and customers, to handle the process competently and appropriately, and she did. The managers and some of the employees sent her notes of appreciation.

Although she didn't enjoy it, this process may have been good for her, giving her something to do and occupying her mind as she tried to adjust to the loss of Brad and to her changed life.

You may have wondered about the inheritance and Brad's brother and his mother. You may have wondered, but Alma didn't. If Brad had wanted he'd have put them in his will. It's possible that his mother was dead and Brad knew it but had never mentioned it to Alma; that's one possibility. Come to think of it, it's quite possible that his brother was dead, too, considering his long term intense relationship with alcohol.

Anyway, that wasn't the issue; the issue was what in the world was Alma going to do now.

ALMA AT THE LIBRARY AFTER BRAD DIED

After Brad's death, and the cruise, and clearing up the businesses, Alma again had the old feeling of loose ends. Her only interests were the gym, walking and reading. And she had no one to talk with. She kept up her appearance as always, but she changed her look. She started wearing her hair shorter, which required less attention, her clothing became more casual, and she used even less makeup than before. She began spending more time in the library, and to her surprise, eventually volunteered there, first a half-day a week, and then two half-days, re-shelving books.

Volunteering came with some perks. She could keep books out as long as she wanted and with no fine no matter how late she returned them. But Alma finished a book in three days unless she lost interest and gave up, so this perk was of no benefit to her. Earlier in life, she'd felt committed to finishing any book she started but she'd realized there was no reason for this. Another perk suited her well though. She got second shot, after the librarians, at any new book before it was shelved. This was, of course, against the rules, but it was part of the culture at this library.

Alma became so knowledgeable about the library and the locations of the books, like her father with the streets of the town, that the less experienced librarians began consulting her for directions.

Alma was reshelving books in the extensive transportation section, a gift from the estate of an eccentric gentleman who'd loved trains. At this moment, she wasn't actually reshelving but was enjoying a book of pictures of early locomotives. She was startled by a tap on her shoulder. It was the head librarian. The lady was a little under middle-age, always wore pants suits and a big floppy bow tie, minimal makeup, and small lensed reading glasses on a chain around her neck. She would've been nice-looking if she hadn't been extremely thin. Alma noticed for the first time that she was wearing a wedding ring and felt slightly pleased for her.

"Alma, may I speak to you for a moment?"

"Of course. Have I done something wrong?"

"No, no. Not at all. In fact, you've been an outstanding volunteer. You've never missed a shift, you're punctual, and you know the library layout as well as any of us. I want to offer you a part-time job."

Alma was startled again.

"A job? Oh, a job."

"Yes. It'd be slightly less than half-time so you wouldn't get insurance or any benefits, and I'm afraid we can't pay much; we just don't have the money. But I'd like to hire you. And maybe we could do better next year."

"Oh, you don't need to pay me. I'd like the job, but I don't need a salary."

Alma felt honored by the offer. As far as she knew, no other volunteer had ever been offered a job. And the idea gave her a sense of belonging, of being a part of something, along with a sense of purpose, all of which had been missing since Brad's death, although Alma hadn't been consciously aware of that.

The head librarian was concerned about Alma's response.

"Well, we need to be clear. You'd be expected to keep your shifts, and follow the rules, and there's a mandatory training before you officially start. I would need to pay you a salary, though. I think it's required if you're employed."

"I really don't want a salary." Alma noticed the confused look on the librarian's face. "Oh, well, I guess if you have to pay me, I can just donate it to the library."

The librarian was puzzled by Alma's position, but she didn't question it further.

"How nice. That's a very nice thing for you to do. Can you come by my office in the morning? I'll have the paperwork ready, and we can schedule you for the training."

"Of course," Alma said. "Thank you."

Later, Alma wondered, "Why was I so quick to take the job? Maybe I should've thought about it first. Hmm. But it feels good to me." Introspection takes some self-confidence. This was a new skill. So she was already realizing some benefit from the job.

Alma was volunteering ten hours a week, and the job was eighteen, just short of eligibility for benefits. In fact, other than the salary she didn't want, the only tangible benefit to the job was now she'd get first shot at new books instead of second shot. But there was a pride in being official, and wearing that blue badge instead of the yellow badge of a volunteer.

The training, in library science and security, which she'd never thought about before, was interesting. She didn't like medical things so she wasn't interested in the first aid sessions but she sailed through them.

Over the next few weeks, most of the staff found occasion to welcome and congratulate her. They liked Alma because she was helpful, efficient and reliable, although there was the occasional comment, "She's not exactly warm and fuzzy, is she?"

On an afternoon several months later Alma was in the stacks reshelving and she smelled smoke. She quickly traced it to the men's restroom. Smoke was pouring from under the door. She didn't hesitate just because it was the men's; she rushed in and saw Ben, who she knew somewhat, sitting on a toilet with his pants around his ankles, smoking. But that wasn't the big problem; Ben had been strangely oblivious to the actual fire in one of the large green trash cans. Well, maybe not so strange; in addition to his cigarette habit Ben had a tendency to drink a bit.

Alma had previously befriended Ben, who spent a lot of time in the library. He was a large Teddy Bear type with an unkempt black beard, who wore a large heavy overcoat at all times, in all seasons. This wasn't as strange as it sounds because the library was kept at a cool temperature, but it must've looked odd outside during the summer. The coat wasn't always clean. Actually, it was never clean. Ben usually wore a purplish knit cap, but whenever he took it off, his hair was strikingly wild. Ben looked like someone who was homeless, which he was.

Ben's overly large coat had huge pockets on the outside and smaller ones on the inside. He had a system and he knew what was in each pocket. One was for his miniatures; he preferred vodka but would take whatever was cheapest. In another he could carry a book if it wasn't too large; many of the books he liked were too large and too heavy. In another pocket were cigarettes, cigarette butts, and matches, and another was for papers - notes he'd made, advertisements, articles he'd torn from discarded magazines, whatever caught his interest. Ben had slit the lining of his coat and inserted old magazines and folded newspapers for armor against knife attacks. He'd never been attacked with a knife but he knew friends who had been, and you couldn't be too careful. And in the winter, the paper stuff was additional insulation against the cold. All of these things made the coat bulky and heavy but Ben was a big man and that didn't bother him. The extra safety and insulation made it worth it.

Ben had sometimes asked Alma to help him find particular books, and she'd recognized his intelligence and intellectual curiosity. He was interested in science and seemed to have some understanding of modern physics, even of quantum mechanics. Many of the books she got for him, such as *Introduction to LaPlace Transforms*, and *Short Impulses, Dirac's Delta Function, and Partial Fractions*, had titles beyond her comprehension and were so esoteric that Alma could only get them through the interlibrary loan system. Ben always returned books on time and undamaged, which must've been a challenge living on the streets.

Although he hadn't told Alma, or anyone, Ben had been a successful engineer before his wife died and he turned to drink. He had a vague plan to get sober and employed again, but he realized that the longer he was out of work and the older he got, the smaller his chances were. Still, he was trying and he appreciated Alma's help as well as her paying him some attention. Homeless people expect to get ignored.

One afternoon Alma had noticed Ben being harassed by one of the security guards even though he wasn't causing any trouble. She'd intervened although she was only a volunteer at the time. She persuaded Ben to leave quietly and she'd managed to handle the situation without offending either the guard or Ben. The next time Ben came in, he was sober, and he looked Alma up and thanked her. They almost had something of a bond.

Anyway, the issue right now was the fire. Ben often smoked in the bathroom, but he'd always been careful to run his cigarette butts under the faucet before putting them in the wastebasket. Unfortunately, he was slightly inebriated today and he'd failed to do that.

"Ben! Put that cigarette out and get out of here! Now!"

Ben looked up, saw the fire, stood and pulled up his pants. He held them up with one hand without pausing to buckle his belt, tossed his cigarette into the sink, and pushed past Alma and out the door, stumbling a bit. I think if he'd been sober he would've tried to help with the fire and to protect Alma, but none of us really knows how we'll react in an emergency, and anyway, he wasn't sober.

Alma momentarily considered pulling the fire alarm as she'd been trained to do, but she knew where all the fire extinguishers were, and she'd been taught how to operate them. She got the nearest extinguisher and quickly put out the fire. By then the smoke had attracted a security guard, not the one who'd harassed Ben, and several of the staff. They shook Alma's hand, clapped her on the back, which she didn't appreciate, and congratulated her. The head librarian arrived and thanked Alma profusely. No one mentioned that she'd been supposed to pull the fire alarm.

The head librarian asked Alma if she knew how the fire had started or if she'd seen anyone in or near the restroom, and, without thinking, Alma said "No. No, I just smelled smoke and when I came in the fire was pretty big."

Later, Alma wondered for a moment why she'd lied. She must've been somewhat fond of Ben. The next time she saw him, she did lecture him and told him that if he kept smoking in the restroom he could be barred from the library. Ben was appropriately contrite and swore it would never happen again. Of course, he continued smoking in the restroom, but he was much more careful from then on. He did come into the library inebriated another time when Alma was on duty and when she told him to leave he did without argument.

Alma thought it strange that she was somewhat attracted to Ben, not in a romantic and certainly not in a sexual way, but in a friendly way. He was obviously intelligent and he was diligent about his reading, and she admired that. He was always polite to her and he was obviously grateful for her help. She was surprised that she enjoyed helping him. Alma thought that after raising her siblings she'd done all the helping she ever wanted to do except when she got monetary reward, as when she'd help dress shop customers. Now she realized that she also enjoyed helping the customers in the library, not only Ben. She didn't give these ideas or feelings much thought, but she was aware of them.

But once again back to the fire. Alma's clothes and hair smelled of smoke, and she asked the head librarian if she could go home to change. The librarian said, "Of course. And take the rest of the day off; we'll still pay you for the full shift."

The next time Alma was on duty, the head librarian told her they'd found some more money and were going to give her a raise. She apparently didn't remember or didn't believe that Alma wasn't interested in the money, or maybe she just couldn't think of any other way to acknowledge her. Alma, of course, didn't want the raise, but she decided it wasn't worth arguing about, and she just said, "Thank you." She still donated all of her salary back to the library.

Alma worked in the library for the rest of her life, and after she gained seniority, she suggested and helped create a number of programs, some especially for the homeless. She also suggested some changes in the arrangements of the books and in the signage, making it easier for people to find things, and this was highly appreciated. She appreciated the appreciation.

Soon after the fire, Alma was promoted to the front desk. She came to know the frequent customers, as she'd known her customers in the dress shop so long ago. She liked answering their questions and eventually she began suggesting specific books that she thought might fit their interests. She became quite popular and her advice was sought after: "Alma, what are you recommending today?" "Which of these do you think would be good for me?" "Have you read this? What did you think of it?"

Alma was able to help some readers expand their horizons, as Anthony had done for her, and like Anthony, she found this gratifying, seeing them enjoying new interests and growing, at least in this small way.

Alma briefly considered buying a book shop. She imagined herself getting acquainted with the customers and offering these same services there. She'd carry only good books but mostly inexpensive, including paperbacks and used books, for customers not so well off. Then she realized that she'd already owned a bookstore, Brad's, and she'd been happy to get rid of it. She'd done enough owning and managing and she was happy at the library. She dropped the idea.

Thinking of bookstores got Alma thinking about Brad's death and his will, and she decided to have had one drawn up. She remembered the high fees associated with Brad's and she used a different firm.

She still liked going to the coffee shop. It had been remodeled only once and still had the old look and atmosphere, and she still enjoyed chats with Arnid, the now owner/manager. Alma occasionally offered a small suggestion about the staff, or the menu, or the décor. Arnid implemented some of them and resented none since Alma offered them tactfully, as she'd learned in the dress shop.

Alma thought it would be nice to include Arnid in her will, not with a lot of money but enough to matter. The rest would go to the library, and now you can see where they're building the new wing with half of it. The other half would go into a trust fund for the employees. They'd be ensured at least minimum wage plus ten percent and a yearly increase tied to the cost of living index but at least one percent. If the library ever closed, the trust would be liquidated and the funds donated to the nearest high school.

She put a lot of thought into her will. She'd read three different books with quite different perspectives about Mary Baker Eddy, the genius who founded Christian Science. Alma greatly admired Ms. Eddy for her intellect, if not her theology, and like her, made sure her will was airtight and impermeable to any meddling, in legalese, in perpetuity.

Alma felt relieved when her will was completed because she now had a small fortune, or maybe a large one, depending on your viewpoint, and you never knew what was going to happen, as we shall soon see.

WHAT HAPPENED TO ALMA'S SISTER, TWO

Alma was sipping white wine and reading a novel when she was interrupted by the telephone.

Her number was on an ID card in Two's purse and the hospital gave it to the state police who called Alma. The drunk driver had hit their car head-on. Two and the drunk died instantly and the boyfriend died on the way to the hospital. Alma's niece was kept alive for ten days until they unhooked her after getting Alma's permission as next of kin. Alma was saddened by the losses, but she got over it quickly.

The hospital billed her for the little girl's care but Alma explained that she had no responsibility for that. She explained several times, over the phone and in writing. The amount was of course obscenely high. It wouldn't have been much for Alma, but she refused to pay it on principle. They continued to bill her and when she stopped responding at all, they sent the bill to a collection agency. The agency harassed her even after she explained the situation and details to them more than once and assured them that she wasn't going to pay.

The agency threatened to sue her and she threatened to report and sue them. One man became abusive on the phone, threatening and using foul language. Alma told him she was recording the conversation, which she wasn't, and then advised him to go perform an anatomically impossible sexual act. Then she slammed the receiver down. That was the last call from the collectors and that apparently was that.

Alma's hair turned an attractive gray. She never considered dying it as many of her contemporaries did. She looked about her age, sixties, then seventies, or maybe a little younger than her age, and that was fine with her as long as she looked her best.

Alma became fascinated with Mary, Queen of Scots. Mary believed she'd been cheated out of the English throne by her cousin Elizabeth. When Mary insisted on her right to the throne Elizabeth persecuted her. Mary was vociferously persistent and didn't offer the Queen the deference she felt entitled to. Then she instigated at least one rebellion and eventually an assassination plot, so finally Elizabeth had Cousin Mary's head chopped off, Mary voicing her right to the throne right up to the bloody en-.

Alma read eight or nine books about Mary and watched several related movies on the library's computer, which attests to the intensity of her interest as she disliked movies and wasn't fond of computers. She was aware that if Brad had been around they'd have had lots of discussion on the Mary history but she did get satisfaction from pursuing it herself.

When she'd mastered the Mary literature and movies, Alma felt sated about her "tocaya" (Spanish for people who share the same first name) and never read any more about Cousin Mary. However, she was always willing to discuss or recommend books about Mary to any interested library patrons, and there were a few, especially some of the Catholic women.

Alma then turned her remarkable focus to learning about the huge effect of illusions in human life and she became expert on the topic. Her favorites were:

- the illusion that we ourselves will never die, although we feel for those poor bastards around us who obviously will and so often do;

- the illusion that our decisions are made consciously and rationally when in fact they're largely made unconsciously based on emotion, and then adorned with reasons after the fact;

- the illusion that people can understand each other, based on the illusion that words mean the same thing to them as they do to us, and that what we say is perfectly clear;

- and the illusion that our memories are accurate, because we remember many things clearly and distinctly. Science proves that we only record certain points of an event and on recall our imagination fills in the rest. The memory is stored away again, modified by our remembering. When we recall it again, it will be different, but we'll still be certain of its accuracy. Eyewitness testimony is notoriously unreliable.

Alma enjoyed sharing these illusions with her patrons whenever an opportunity arose. They tended to not believe her, being firmly attached to the illusion that their illusions were not illusions at all. Alma handled these discussions so tactfully that they never devolved into arguments. But occasionally, a patron would return and say they'd been thinking about the ideas or even read one of the books Alma had suggested, and acknowledge that there might be something to what Alma had told them. These rare incidents of enlightenment were particularly gratifying. Alma didn't see how these concepts might apply to her and so her knowledge about them had little effect on her. Well, OK, not any.

Alma learned that higher animals can think and problem solve, and have dreams and emotions, but that there's no evidence that any animals other than humans have illusions. "That's funny," she thought.

After illusions, Alma moved on. She immersed herself in one topic at a time until she'd mastered it, while simultaneously enjoying fiction. She never lost interest in a favorite puzzle from her illusion phase, "If I say something's purple and you agree, are we actually experiencing the same color?" Few patrons were interested in this topic and a few looked at her strangely if she brought it up, so she didn't often, and she never found an answer to that question.

Alma learned all she wanted about Tibet and hadn't picked up a new topic yet when one fell in her lap, if it's possible for a topic to do that. And she did find some answers, some interesting ones. But first, before she got engrossed in the new topic, she got involved in a situation.

THE ACCIDENT: ALMA AS A PARAMEDIC

Alma had no interest in medical things, so she'd been unenthusiastic about the library's first aid course and never imagined actually using it. The training turned out to be a good thing, however.

On a Saturday morning walk, Alma heard a crash and then screaming. She rounded the corner and saw that a young girl, maybe ten years old, had crashed her bicycle. The sharp edge of the bike pedal had cut a big gash behind her knee. The girl was lying next to the bike, holding her leg and screaming. Blood was spurting out and her shorts were already soaked. Alma knew that an artery was cut and that this was serious.

Alma dropped to her knees by the girl and pressed her hand on the wound.

"You'll be OK. You'll be OK," she said to the screaming girl. She scanned the bystanders, a boy and a girl standing gaping next to their bikes and a man and a woman standing and staring. "Are you all with her?" she asked.

The children nodded yes, and the adults said, "No, no. No."

Then she asked, "Who has a cell phone?" The adults and the boy raised their hands. She pointed to the man, "Call 911. Now. Now!"

She turned to the boy, "Give me your shirt."

He took a step back. "What?" he exclaimed.

"Your shirt. Take it off. Give me your shirt. Now."

Slowly, the boy did. Fortunately, it wasn't cold and he was wearing a T undershirt.

The girl's screams had subsided to whimpers and she lay very still on the ground. Alma folded the boy's shirt and put it on the wound and again applied pressure. Soon the shirt was soaked.

"You'll be OK," Alma said again. "You'll be OK."

She asked the children, "Are you her brother and sister?" The boy looked about twelve and the girl about seven or eight, so they could've been. They shook their heads no.

"Do you know where she lives?"

The girl nodded yes and the boy said, "Yeah."

"You two go get her parents. OK?"

The children nodded but just stood there.

"Get on your bikes and go to her house and get her parents. Bring them here. Now. Go. Go!"

The children jumped on their bikes and raced off.

Alma asked the man, "Did you get 911?"

"Yep, they're coming," he said and started walking away. The woman stood still and watched him go.

Alma didn't blame the children for anything although she wondered if they might've been involved in the accident. But once again, she was amazed at the stupidity of adults. Well, not amazed because she observed this frequently, but at least mildly surprised.

The parents arrived soon, and the ambulance immediately after. The parents stood there looking and the mother kept asking, "What happened? What happened?"

She looked pale and woozy. Alma wondered if she might've had a few nips, although it was early in the day, but her appearance could just as easily have been explained by the fact that it was her child and there was a lot of blood.

The EMT brusquely moved Alma away from the girl, but he did say "Good job, lady." He got bandages from a pack and applied pressure to the wound just as Alma had been. His female partner, whom Alma thought she recognized from her own previous accident, was busy getting the stretcher; she didn't look at Alma and Alma didn't speak to her.

Alma stood to the side and watched for a moment. She had a fleeting memory of when she'd skinned her knee as a child. A bike accident then too, but not nearly that much blood, and nobody, nobody, had been saying, "You'll be OK; you'll be OK."

"Anyway," she thought, "That was a long time ago and just a skinned knee. It wasn't anything. Nothing at all," and then she remembered that she was planning to get to the library soon. "

I want to see if that new book by Kingsolver is in yet so I can get it before somebody else does."

She didn't want to miss the Kingsolver book; more importantly, she didn't want to have to deal with the parents giving her effusive thanks and all that crap, although she realized that possibly they'd express no gratitude at all, but she wasn't going to take the risk.

She walked off, continuing her route. And that was that.

ALMA GETS INTERESTED IN HER FAMILY AGAIN

OK, we got sidetracked by the little girl and her accident, and Alma's memories, but we'd been on the subject of Alma finding a new topic of interest and finding some answers. This is gonna be good.

One warm summer afternoon Alma was behind the desk in the library, somewhat bored. The library wasn't busy, hopefully because many of the patrons were outdoors enjoying the weather.

One of her clientele walked in and Alma was glad to see her. The woman said a friendly hello and then asked, "What are you?"

Alma was puzzled. "What do you mean?"

"Well, I'm kind of excited. I just got my DNA report and I'm mostly Irish, in my genes anyway. My parents were both from Denmark and I figured that's where we went back to but no, I'm Irish and Scandinavian. So I looked up the history and the Vikings raided Ireland a lot way back and they took some of the Irish captives back home with them, so see, that's how it could've happened."

Alma said, "That's interesting," just to be polite, because frankly, she didn't find it interesting but, encouraged, the lady went on about what she'd found and about the process. She was quite excited. Alma was learning more than she'd ever wanted to know about genealogy. The lady told her that after she got her DNA results, she'd gotten on ancestry.com, and she was enjoying looking up ancestors and filling in her family tree.

Alma was pleased for her client with her new interest, but she couldn't imagine doing anything like that herself. It didn't seem interesting and she disliked spending time on computers, although she'd been using the library's more.

Then she had a dream that, unlike usually, she remembered the next morning. In the dream her great Grandma, Grandma Alma, was smiling and holding out a handful of candy, saying, "Alma, Alma, take it, take it." The dream restimulated her curiosity about Grandma Alma.

The next week the genealogy lady returned and Alma asked her about the research process. She eventually sent her saliva for DNA testing. She figured it was inexpensive and after all, what could it hurt?

Surprise! The report said she not only had Western European genes, and some Scandinavian, like the lady patron, but she also had Jewish genes. Alma had never imagined that but it was interesting enough that she got on the computer and went to the ancestry.com site.

She wasn't trying to do her family tree; she just wanted to learn about her Grandma Alma, and maybe about her other grandparents. This was surprisingly easy to do. Wonderfully, a woman relative, a genealogy nut, had researched the family and posted information about Grandma Alma. Unfortunately, the genealogy nut died or she might've posted more or Alma might even have tried to get in touch with her.

Grandma Alma wasn't a little bit Spanish as her mother had said. Not a little bit Spanish, she was Spanish. And Jewish. And her Hebrew name, Neshama, like Alma in Spanish, means soul. That explained why her mother said they called her Nessie. Alma's ancestors had been conversos, Jews who'd "converted" to Catholicism to avoid the persecutions of the inquisition.

Alma was mainly interested in her great grandma, but she was curious enough to enter her other grandparents into the program. They were just Scandinavian, no interesting mixtures. There was no other information about them except she learned that she had an Aunt Ingrid, who was still alive and whom she'd never heard of, of course. The only thing she'd ever heard about her father's family was that they lived on the west coast and wanted nothing to do with her family or with her.

On her mother's side, her Jewish family had been fortunate. They hadn't been tortured or burned at the stake but simply had all their assets confiscated and distributed among the church officials, and been driven from Spain. They settled in Holland for a generation; when the persecution became too severe there they fled to Mexico. They found The Inquisition awaiting them there too. Not wishing to undergo the harsh consequences of their Jewishness, they converted to Catholicism.

Alma was focused on her great grandmother, but she couldn't help visualizing generations of her family trudging across Europe pulling wooden carts carrying their meager belongings or helplessly standing watching their homes burn. She had an unfamiliar feeling, sympathy, thinking of this.

Alma found the conversos fascinating, these people who'd had such drastic changes in their lives and who had such secrets.

In Mexico, over time most of her family became fervent Catholics. They either gave up their Jewishness or kept it hidden. But the Inquisition was persistently inquisitive, as well as land and gold hungry, and many of the family didn't feel safe in Mexico. They migrated north, along El Camino Real de Tierra Adentro, to what is now New Mexico, praying every step of the way to the patron saint of the trail, the Santo Nino de la Atocha. In private some of them were also praying to Adonai. It wasn't an easy trip.

I would say `praying to Yahweh' here, but my friend Victor says that term is too holy to speak and the family would've used, Adonai, meaning the Lord.

Other Jewish friends told me that nowadays most Jews would just say God, but we aren't talking about nowadays. Those ancestors struggling up the El Camino, praying for a better life in New Mexico, wouldn't have used the Y word or "God." No, it was Adonai for sure. And it worked; they got to New Mexico.

New Mexico was part of Mexico until 1846. Then our eleventh president, James K. Polk, declared that the United States had a "manifest destiny" to expand and he invaded Mexico. The US Army won every battle, including the one against Los Niños Héroes, teenage military cadets who died defending Mexico City`s Chapultepec Castle. This story was particularly poignant for Alma.

Mexico lost about one-third of its territory, including New Mexico. And guess what? The Inquisition was in New Mexico also. Since this wasn't the haven the family had hoped, successive generations dispersed over the country.

Alma had never been interested in history, politics, or any religion, but she got hooked on researching Grandma Alma and her family. She became an expert on the conversos. She was surprised by her feeling for these people whom she'd never met, and of course, never would.

Many of the converso descendants had no knowledge of or connection to their background, except in their genes. Some still practiced family traditions that they didn't realize were Jewish; some knowingly practiced Judaism in secret.

Grandma Alma was a devout Catholic and attended mass daily. But every Friday night, she lit candles; no one ever understood why. When she was asked about it, all she could say, or maybe all she would say, was that her mother had always done it.

Those who knew they were Jewish also knew that though The Inquisition was gone, bigotry and stigma weren't, and so for business and cultural reasons, they still kept their Jewishness hidden. Thus Alma's family tradition of secrecy and closed mouthedness. Alma wondered if her Catholic mother had even known that she was Jewish.

Are there genes for secrecy? Being Jewish was dangerous, so natural selection would favor those genes being passed on. Or maybe it was just the culture of secrecy that favored survival and that was passed down through the family.

Alma learned about secrecy among the conversos and about the possible role of genetics. But the genetics were confusing and frustrating so she didn't pursue them and neither will we. "Thank God," I can imagine you saying, or perhaps, "Thank Adonai."

Alma realized that she was more wary and private than the average person, and she wondered if that was from the family secrecy thing. From her reading she knew that many families were more open and more connected than hers had been, but that didn't appeal to her, in fact, it repelled her. "Touchy feelie," she labeled it. But she felt a connection with her deceased Grandma, more than she'd felt with her living family members. "Strange," she thought.

The only information about Grandma Alma's husband, or husbands, was that Grandma had outlived all three of them. Alma admired that. And there was no information about Grandma's children. Was Alma's mother an only child? Alma remembered her mother saying she was told to keep the candy secret or `they'd all want one.' Who was "all?" Was the habit of secrecy so strong it was automatically applied to everything?

Alma was pleased to finally learn about her great grandmother. She got more comfortable using the computer for research, but she never got involved in social media; not her thing.

She still knew nothing about her father's family, but even that veil of secrecy would finally be pierced.

A NEW PHASE OF ALMA'S LIFE AND MORE ABOUT HER FAMILY

Years later, Alma's reading was interrupted by a memory of the lobster man. Why? Was she lonely? He'd been nice. She couldn't remember his name. Henry? That didn't seem right, but she couldn't think of any other possibility. She hoped he was well and successful in his lobster niche and had met the right woman. She had no inclination to look him up.

So maybe she wasn't that lonely.

A few days later, Alma suddenly remembered. The day of her lobster man remembrance one of her patrons had asked for a book suggestion. The lady wanted to try a new direction.

Alma thought a moment, "Well, have you read Gabriel?"

"Gabriel?"

"*Love in the Time of Cholera? 100 Years of Solitude?*"

"No. Never heard of them. What are they like?"

"Well, they're different. Some people don't like them but *Love in the Time of Cholera* is one of my favorites. I think you'd like it."

The lady nodded. "Thanks. I'll go get it. It's time for me to do something different, open my mind. This is probably about as wild as I'll ever get though."

The lady returned. "I can't find those books anywhere."

Alma thought for a minute. "Whoops! It's not Gabriel; it's Gabriel Garcia Marquez. Go look under Garcia Marquez."

Soon the lady was back waving *Cholera* in one hand and *100 Years* in the other. "I think I'll try Cholera first `cause you said it's your favorite. If I like it, I'll try the other one before they're due."

"Good thinking. I think you'll like them both. I hope so."

"Well, I hope so, too. Thanks a lot. You've never steered me wrong."

When Alma remembered that incident, it all made sense. The lobster man's mother had recommended Garcia Marquez to her; for some reason, she'd always thought of him as Gabriel. She'd need to correct that. But the point was, this explained why she'd thought of lobster man, and she was glad, because it proved that the remembrance hadn't anything to do with her being lonely; she wasn't lonely at all. She was busy and satisfied. And independent. It was good to be sure about that.

For a moment, she thought she might write the mother a note of gratitude. That would be a nice gesture, and maybe she could even inquire about lobster man. But this was absurd. She didn't have the address, although she could easily find it but the old lady might be dead, and what would be the point anyway? It would've definitely been unAlmaish. So that was that, and she probably never thought of lobster man again, although maybe she briefly did, whenever those books came up. But that didn't mean that she was lonely, it was just a connection in her mind with the Garcia Marquez books. See, she got the name right that time.

Alma was walking less, drinking less, reading more, and going to bed earlier. She still got to the gym three times a week, and still kept to herself there, just attending to business. Occasionally a new client would try to engage her but they'd back off when Alma clearly and politely, never rudely nor crudely, wasn't interested. By now she was one of the older exercisees, some of whom, like Alma, did significant workouts and others who apparently just came to socialize and occasionally make a desultory pass at some of the equipment.

Alma was enjoying the patrons at the library. She'd built up a clientele as she had at the dress shop, but without the insincerity. She enjoyed talking with them and wasn't in a hurry to end the conversations.

She decided to call the aunt she'd discovered on the genealogy site. The aunt was probably old and if Alma was ever going to try to find her, sooner might be wiser than later. Alma had learned enough about Grandma Alma, but she'd like to learn something about her father's side.

Googling got her a phone number. The phone was answered on the first ring, and it was her aunt Ingrid, who spoke perfect English with a British accent. She wasn't excited to hear from Alma but she was civil. That seemed British-like, too. Alma explained why she was calling and that she'd only just learned about the woman's existence, though that wasn't quite true. The woman said she hadn't known about Alma either.

After a pause, Alma said she was hoping to learn something about her grandparents. "My parents never would tell me about my great Grandma or any of the rest of the family."

"Of course not," the woman said, "And I'm not even supposed to be talking to you."

"What!?" Alma exclaimed.

"In my family, your family is taboo."

"What in the world?"

There was a long silence and then the aunt said, "Your father was disowned when he married your mother. Our family comes from a long line of shipbuilders. They were well off and they thought your mother was beneath them. And even worse, they suspected she might have some Jewish blood."

"She did have," Alma replied. "She did. What about that?"

Silence again. Then the woman spoke.

"Well, I know times have changed, but back then, that wasn't acceptable. So when your father insisted on marrying that woman, the family cut him off, cut them both off."

"My! How sad. What else can you tell me?"

Silence again.

Then, "Well. I remember one argument about the marriage when your father was talking about love and my father shouted, `We are a family of shipbuilders, not damned poets!' and slammed his coffee mug down on the table so hard that he broke the mug and left a dent in the table. My mother was furious about both the mug and the dent. But she cleaned up the mug and the coffee without saying anything. That dent is still in the table today."

Pause.

"That's all I know, that's all," the aunt said. "Sorry, I'm busy. I have to ring off now."

She hung up. Alma was stunned. She sat with her thoughts for a while and then went on with other pursuits. She didn't do any more genealogy research or fill in any more blanks on the ancestry site. She'd discovered enough about her grandparents and she was satisfied.

And that was that.

OUR FINAL INTERLUDE

As he finished telling me about Alma's family stuff, my friend started coughing, hard, and gasping for breath. It was a little scary.

"You OK?" I asked.

He caught his breath. "Yeah. Something went down the wrong way, you know. I'm fine. Gotta go pee. Don't you dare touch my drink while I'm gone."

"Don't need to, got my own. You gonna be all right? You've had a few."

"You're one to talk. No reason for you to give me a raft of shit about booze. You've been going pretty steady yourself, you know?"

"Yeah, guess so." I choked back a snide comment, that I hadn't started drinking for breakfast yet, and just asked, "Think you can find your way back?"

"Humph," he threw back over his shoulder as he walked off. He seemed OK, steady, walking in a straight line. Some people can drink like that, not me. I was already feeling a little buzzed, like maybe I should slow down if not stop.

While he was gone, I sat staring into my half empty glass. I got lost in my thoughts. I've always been fascinated by the English language. When I say "my old friend," does that mean my friend of long-standing, or my friend who has attained many years, or, as in this case, both? And how could you tell which it meant if I hadn't told you? You might be wondering why I'd be old friends with this guy who at times seems brusque, to put it gently. Well, believe it or not, he's a pretty nice guy when he's sober, tho that seems to be occurring less and less these days. We've had lots of conversations about books, more interesting because we rarely agree. And apparently, now we share, how shall I say, an interest, in Alma, who was growing on me more the more I heard.

Thinking about Alma got me thinking about my wife, my late wife, as they say, who I loved dearly, even though she could be difficult at times; those last two comments are both understatements. I was starting to feel nostalgic, a feeling I don't relish, but it's another signal that I've had about enough to drink. I'd learned that the hard way.

I forced my thoughts back to Alma. I was starting to feel attached to this woman somehow, a woman I'd never even met. I couldn't figure out why, but she had a good story. I was sorry to realize that her story was about to end. Maybe my ending wouldn't come too far behind. But I bet I'll at least get to see the library addition finished, the addition named for her. She must've been quite a gal.

It occurred to me that maybe my old friend had been in love with Alma. Certainly he was a lonely guy, that's partly why he spends so much time in the bar. It sounds like Alma was lonely too, although apparently she'd never admit it. I have no trouble admitting I'm lonely; I miss my wife a lot. I was starting to feel nostalgic again and I was glad when my friend came back and interrupted me before it got any worse.

I jumped when he clapped me on the shoulder and yelled in my ear, "Hey! Hey bozo, come back to earth! Don't pass out on me, you bald-headed old fart. You wimpy college pukes never could hold your liquor."

I knew that my friend had a college degree, but in what? Engineering? He'd made his money in commercial real estate, quite a lot I believe. He must've had some kind of problem in school because he'd never talk about it and he despised college faculty, "inept impotent intellectuals," he liked to call them, uhmm, us.

If you'll indulge me for a moment, I'd like to clarify that I'm only partially bald; my wife used to say it was sexy. In fact, I have more hair than my friend does. And by the way, I may be old, but my old friend's older than me. Just saying.

Anyway, he kept on, "And don't start talking about my drinking. I had enough of that crap with my wives, you know? What a bunch!"

"OK, OK. Anyway, nobody touched your drink; the ice hasn't even melted much, so why don't you go on and finish the story?"

"Right." He lifted his drink and held it to the light to examine it, swirling the liquor so that the ice made a pleasant clinking sound; then he took a big swallow. "You know, I spent a fair amount of time with her, with Alma, there at the library, you know. I mean she was one of the reasons I spent so much time there. She was good to talk to and she was always nice, not like a lot of people, you know, no offense. I mean, spending time there had to be better than spending time here with jerks like you and that stupid bartender for company, don't you think?"

I estimated he had a pretty good load on by now and I wanted to hear the rest of Alma's story before he got worse. "Yeah, sounds about right. You got pretty close to her?"

"No, no, I couldn't say that. I mean when I started hanging round there she was kinda distant, you know? But she warmed up some, or opened up some, maybe not warm. Don't you go getting the idea that I had a crush on her or anything. Hell, I've been way too old for that stuff for years. Shit, I couldn't do anything anyway even if the opportunity should arise, if you get my drift, no pun etcetera. But you know, she was good looking, decent, intelligent, and she knew books. That's what we talked about mostly, books."

"Mostly?"

"Well, you know, after a while, I started telling her about me, my divorces, my kids, how the little bastards mostly won't have anything to do with me. Grown up little bastards now, I guess. Anyway, I was telling her about all that crap, you know? She was a good listener. And she talked some about her life, losing her husband and all, very sad, must've been a nice guy, young. You ever wonder, how some guys go young, and here we still are, you and me, and for what, you know? For what? You ever wonder?"

"Of course, I think we all do. `Life must go on, I forget just why,' `Ode to an Athlete Dying Young,' that stuff."

"What the hell are you talking about now?"

"You know, poems. Sorry, my literary side gets carried away sometimes."

"OK, fine. Never cared for that poetry crap myself, too fluffy or something, you know?"

I wasn't about to point out to him that these poems were anything but fluffy; I wanted to get back to Alma.

I had plenty of time. Nothing to hurry for. But I slowed down my drinking; I wanted my head to be clear, if it ever was these days, so that I could follow. I was thinking about Alma's story and wondering if maybe I could tell it someday, if I could tell it well. I need to find something more to do with myself now. Yeah, I do miss my wife.

"OK, no poetry. And what about Alma? She started sharing with you?" I was starting to wish that I'd known her, maybe wishing she'd been sharing with me instead of with him.

"Well, that's it, I guess. A coupla days she wasn't at the library and so I asked and they told me she was in the hospital and all, so one day I went over there, you know, but she had a fricking `No Visitors' thing, and I don't know if she woulda wanted to see me anyway. I mean, we weren't close or anything, you know, it's just that I admired her and I enjoyed her company. I guess maybe I was fond of her or something, you know?"

I was thinking that my suspicion about his falling for Alma was being confirmed, but I didn't want to get into his stuff; I wanted to stick with her.

"Yeah, sounds like it. OK, so she shared with you. So how about you share with me what she shared with you?"

"Sure, no secrets here, you know. You manage to get that lazy son of a bitch to come over and give me a refill and I'll fill you in."

So I did, and he did.

ALMA'S LAST PHASE

Once she'd satisfied her curiosity about her family, Alma got kinda stalled. I guess being stuck in a rut isn't the worst thing that can happen to a person, although it has a bad connotation; "stuck," implies that you want to get out of the rut and can't. But Alma wasn't "stuck." Her life was pleasant and she had no desire to change it. Her activities were all optional and were enjoyable or she wouldn't have been doing them. There was the library, gym, walking, reading, and the coffee shop. She also continued to enjoy her half a glass of wine in the evening, occasionally having a nice French red instead of a white. I can see why this might seem like a rut to you, but Alma didn't see it that way and neither do I.

Alma thought she was aging well. Most of us get concerned about that as we reach middle age. She'd probably been less concerned about it than most of us, but she was human. She still noticed admiring glances, mostly from men, but she rarely had to fend off approaches and she never had to be rude or crude to do that.

She had always taken good care of herself. She stayed in good physical condition and kept her weight down. She never dieted but kept healthy eating habits, being blessed, although she never would've said it that way, by never really caring about food. She rarely ate sweets. She never smoked. Her cholesterol and blood pressure were probably good, although she never had them checked. She was quite healthy and had little risk of a stroke, heart attack, or cancer.

But then, you never know.

Alma had another fall and fractured the same leg again, higher up, in the thigh, more serious, especially at her age. Actually, she didn't exactly fall; on her walk she was rounding a corner when a teenage skateboarder came from the other direction. He went down as well. The boy picked himself up, picked up his skateboard, and only then looked at Alma as she lay there dazed but breathing, and then he skateboarded off without a word.

For the second time in her life Alma was rescued by strangers. They called 911 and someone rescued her purse which she'd begun carrying on her walks. It didn't contain much of value, but having to cancel and renew two credit cards and replace the driver's license, which was primarily for identification, would've been a hassle. But as it turned out, it didn't matter.

And for the second time in her life Alma was taken off by ambulance. The EMTs were gentle and quick. She was in some pain although it wasn't bad, not yet, probably because of shock and because it was chilly. Maybe because they were in a hurry, the EMTs didn't put a splint on her leg as they should have. This could've caused serious problems but thankfully didn't. Alma didn't even notice that they didn't use the siren, but they soon got to the emergency room and wheeled her in. Once inside the hallway, the younger EMT shouted, "Femur fracture, vitals stable, elderly," just like on TV, which Alma had never watched. Alma did notice the "elderly." She thought it unnecessary and not entirely accurate; well, maybe slightly accurate.

A nurse yelled, "Trauma Four" and Alma was wheeled into a green-tiled room with large bright lights overhead. Several people in green scrubs were waiting by the table in the center of the room. The nurse entered and directed the others to lift Alma onto the table. She had large scissors and cut Alma's pants leg from her waist to her ankle and flipped it open. "Darn!" thought Alma, "That's a waste."

"Not open," stated the nurse, meaning no bones were sticking through the skin. Meanwhile, someone strapped a blood pressure cuff on her right arm, pumped it too tight, and yelled, "Hundred over sixty." Someone else read the pinchy thing on her finger and yelled, "Ninety-eight," meaning her pulse, of course, usually in the sixties because she was in good shape, and "Sat ninety-six," her oxygen level. Someone else said, "A little pinch now," stuck a needle in her left arm just below the elbow and taped her arm to a small board. Meanwhile, in this organized chaos, a trite term but who could think of a better one, the nurse had put on surgical gloves and was feeling her thigh. "It's maybe two sites, but not displaced," she stated although Alma didn't hear her because the nurse's poking on her leg hurt and Alma couldn't help letting out a scream.

"Sorry. All done." The nurse said, and asked, "Are you in much pain, dear?" Alma realized that "Dear" must be her, and said, "A little, well, yes, it's getting worse."

"OK," the nurse said, "We'll get you something. You're going to be OK." Not entirely accurate, but this couldn't have been known one way or the other this early in the game.

The nurse barked out orders. "Georgia, get the orthopod on call in here, stat. Frank, set up X-ray, left femur, AP and lateral, stat. Then get the pit boss for some pain control. Samantha, get that inflatable splint on, not tight. The EMTs should've done that. Then call the lab in, CBC and diff, metabolic panel, T and C, two units whole blood. Georgia, run in D5W, one liter, to keep open. OK, Jessica, you take over now."

Alma, never interested in medical things, didn't understand the jargon. If you don't either, and if you're particularly interested, some of it gets clarified later and I'd suggest you just keep reading and don't worry about it. The staff knew what it meant and they knew what they were doing.

This team had been working together for some time and each knew their roles, except Frank, a recent nursing school graduate new to the team, so Jessica had known she'd be taking over. She'd been recording all the results and the orders. She said, "Got it. Samantha, be sure the splint's not too tight. When you're done let's wheel her on over to X-ray."

The first nurse patted Alma on the shoulder. "Honey, I'm sorry; it looks like a bad break, but you'll be OK. They're going to give you something for pain and take you to X-ray now. Are you allergic to anything?" Alma was starting to hurt significantly and she was aware of feeling a little scared and a little overwhelmed, but she was mostly aware of how dreadfully cold it was in the room. She said, "No, but I'm awful cold."

"Sorry," said the nurse. "Frank, get her two blankets, warm ones. Let's move, people. I'll check on you later, honey." And she left as they lifted Alma onto a cart and started rolling her out of the room. One of the nurses, Alma assumed it was the one in charge now but couldn't remember her name, Jessica, walked beside her carrying a clipboard, and asked, "What's your name, hon?" and "What medicines are you taking, Alma?" and "Any allergies? Medical problems?"

In the X-ray hall, Alma only had to wait a few minutes before the X-ray tech came up. `Hi, I'm Fiona, gonna take a picture of your leg. OK?"

Alma's "OK," came out softer and hoarser than she'd intended, so she repeated it. "OK."

Frank showed up with two warm blankets and put them nicely over her, even tucking her feet in. He gave her a paper cup with two pills in it and another with a little water. After she took the pills, Frank and Fiona wheeled her into the X-ray room and lifted her onto the table. Because now there were only the two of them, they couldn't be as gentle as before and it hurt. "Damn!" exclaimed Alma. "Easy, please."

Fiona patted her good leg and said, "Sorry, you're good now. Now be real still and I'll tell you when to hold your breath."

She went into another room and Frank stepped out into the hall. "OK, hold now," Fiona's distorted voice came over a loudspeaker and startled Alma, but she held her breath, heard a click, and Fiona again, "OK, breathe now."

Fiona came back in and helped Alma turn toward her side, propped her there with a pillow, and repeated the process. She returned and said, "You wait just a minute while I check these, but they should be good." She opened the door and waved Frank in from the hall and left again.

"How you doing?" asked Frank.

"OK," Alma replied. "Maybe not great," because she was hurting some and was still cold.

Fiona returned, "Good to go. I'm not supposed to say, but it does look nasty. But you'll be OK. Let's go, you be still and let us move you," and they did, back onto the cart that had been patiently waiting at the side of the room.

"Thanks," said Frank to Fiona, "See ya."

"K." Fiona held the door while Frank wheeled her out. Soon Alma was back in the trauma room and Jessica came in. "You OK?"

"I guess so."

"OK, the orthopod's on the way. Admissions is coming in now; can you talk to them?"

"OK."

"Can I get you anything? Anybody you want called?"

"Yes. No. Nobody to call. I'm thirsty."

"Sure, I'm sorry, but you can't have anything 'til the surgeon decides what to do. Frank, get some toothettes for her lips and a few ice chips. I'm gonna open the IV a little. Alma, are you warm enough?"

Alma appreciated the concern. "No, not really. It's freezing in here."

"I know."

"I'll get some more warm blankets," Frank volunteered. "You sure there's nobody to call?"

"Nobody. Thanks."

Alma wasn't sure whether she was sorry about that or not. It might be nice to have somebody there, but they might've been a bother, too. And the staff was looking after her; she had no complaints except she hoped they wouldn't have to move her again, at least not for a while. And maybe Frank could hurry up with the blankets.

Alma was alone for a few minutes for the first time since she'd entered the ER. Then the admissions lady came in; that's how she introduced herself, "Hello. I'm the admissions lady."

She was tired-looking, middle-aged. Her hair was a mess. She was the first hospital person Alma had seen in street clothes and not green scrubs. Even in her situation and in some pain, Alma noted that she wasn't chewing gum.

"I've got some questions to ask. Let me know if you get too tired or anything, OK?"

Alma was already too tired, but she nodded.

"Do you have some ID with you? That'll make things go faster."

Alma looked bewildered but Frank had returned with blankets, thank goodness. "Her purse is in the bag under the cart."

Alma hadn't been worrying about her purse, but she was glad it was there.

The admissions lady pulled a grocery bag from under the cart and took out a purse. "This yours?"

Alma nodded again. The lady handed it to her, "If you could get some ID and any insurance cards, we'll be rocking."

Alma did. The lady copied down some information, and then, "OK, just a few questions now and we'll wrap it up. OK?"

Alma nodded again.

"We're doing a doubleheader; I'm checking you into the ER and admitting you at the same time, saves time." She got the basic information and then asked about allergies. The lady sounded tired and Alma was getting tired herself.

"I already told them, twice."

"I know, but we need to do it right, to be careful. You'll get asked some more, too. Any allergies?"

"No, no allergies," Alma sighed. "And no medicines, and no medical problems."

"Well, you do know the drill, don't you? OK, I got those. Next of kin?"

"None."

"What? Next of kin?"

"No, no next of kin. None."

"OK. Well, what can I put, who could we contact?"

"You mean if I don't survive?"

"Or whatever. Who could we notify?"

Alma named the head librarian and Arnid from the coffee shop.

"And what are the relationships?

"Employer and ex-employee."

The lady looked dubious. "If you say so. I'll put them down then. Can you give me the phone numbers?"

Although Alma occasionally fleetingly wondered what had become of her presumably surviving sister, she didn't much care; she just hoped things had worked out well for her. So in the ER, her sister never entered her mind, not as next of kin, or as anything.

The lady asked about DNR. Somehow Alma knew about that so she said yes but that she'd never done the paperwork. The lady had her sign a paper but said she'd have to catch her later and have one of the doctors sign it, too.

No, she didn't have a living will. The lady sighed. "I know, you weren't expecting this. You probably can't get that done here, but when you get out, you need to get one done. You got a will?"

"Just a regular will, I guess," replied Alma, feeling chastised and a little foolish."

"Well, that's good," the lady nodded approval. "Good."

Jessica stepped in the door. She was holding a clipboard with a lot of papers on it. "Oh, sorry. I can come back in a few."

"Nope," the admissions lady said. "We're just wrapping up. Alma, I just need you to sign these for HIPPA and insurance and payment. Here and here and here." She handed Alma her clipboard and a pen and then the forms one at a time. Alma signed and handed the stuff back.

The admissions lady looked through the papers and said, "Good. That's it. You're in. If there's anything else I'll catch you later. OK. Good luck, hon."

Then Jessica had more forms to be signed.

Alma didn't know what she'd signed and she didn't care. Alma was tired of the whole business. She just wanted to get to a warm room and go to sleep.

But it wasn't to be. Not yet.

"Well, good morning, young lady," a little too loud and a little too cheerfully, a man bounded into the room wearing green scrubs and one of those funny caps. A facemask was dangling around his neck but no stethoscope. He wasn't bad looking and he seemed friendly, but Alma was beyond caring.

"How you doing? What's your pain level, 0 to 10?"

Alma was feeling somewhat overwhelmed by his approach and she wasn't sure whether zero was none or the worst. "I'm OK, a little pain. I'm still cold."

Alma noticed that he was clean-shaven except for a small white goatee, which struck her as odd-looking.

"OK, OK. Jack, get the lady a couple more blankets. It's bad enough without her having to be cold."

He was actually talking to Frank, who didn't seem to mind the error, at least he didn't say anything but just went off, presumably for even more blankets, hopefully warm ones.

"Young lady, I'm sorry to tell you I've just seen your X-rays and they are ugly, no offense, I mean, ugly. You have a femur fracture in two places, not so good. I've already scheduled the OR. We'll wait three days to let the swelling go down and then we'll go in."

He was palpating her thigh while talking.

"Ouch!" Alma said, but she didn't scream this time.

"Sorry. I'm Dr. Jacoby, surgeon, by the way, the bone man. The good news is that your bones look pretty good; shouldn't be any problems. I guess you exercise and take your vitamin D."

"Yes. No. No vitamins."

"Well, guess you get a lot of sunshine. Or maybe you just have good genes."

Alma snorted, to herself, "Good genes. Yeah, right."

"OK. I'll get the nurses to bring the paperwork for the surgery. From what I see on your X-ray, you're gonna need a rod and a plate. Now you'll be in bed for a while. Be sure to wiggle the toes; let's don't be throwing any clots. But otherwise, keep that leg still; we don't want things slipping around in there."

The surgeon paused and looked at Alma's leg again but he didn't touch it this time. Then he looked around the room for a minute and picked up a mask that someone had dropped on the floor. He wadded it up and tossed it into a nearby trash can, making a pretty good shot. Then he turned back to Alma.

"Any allergies? Medical problems? Give Jack a list of all your medicines. We'll just stop them all unless something is essential. I'll write an order to raise your pain meds, add some PRN. You shouldn't have to hurt any. Well?"

"Well, what?"

"Any allergies? Medical problems? You got any questions?" Too many questions too fast but that was his way, hyper.

Alma was thinking, "This guy is a little too much, but I kind of like him. I hope he's not like Brad's brother. Shouldn't he have asked me before he started feeling around on my leg? I guess that's not important."

"Well?"

"Oh. No. I guess not. And no allergies, no problems."

"OK, gotta run; got another one scheduled. You think of some questions, just ask the nurse. And make sure you keep the pain down and wiggle those toes. And start drinking a lot of water, and you can eat now. Surgery isn't for three days. See you later."

He turned and rushed out the door, nearly bumping into Frank on his way in. "Whoops!" Frank exclaimed. "Excuse me." But the surgeon was already long gone.

"Wow," Alma said to Frank. "He's something."

"Yeah, he is; comes on strong. But he's a good surgeon. Now I'll order you some lunch. You must be hungry."

"Not really. I'm not too much on food."

"OK, I'll bring you a menu and you can see what you'd like. You need to eat a little something. The soup's usually not bad and you want to start with something light anyway. We'll be finding a bed for you, get you out of this cold ER. I'm afraid it can take a while for a bed to open up though. Jessica'll be in with the paperwork and stuff and explain things, and you can ask her any questions. If we start to get busier, we may have to move you out into the hall `til we can get you a room. I hope not though."

And he was gone.

Alma lay there, her thoughts rambling. It was too much all at once, and she wasn't even clear what she wanted to think about. She realized that this ER experience had been different from her first, except the awful cold was the same. But this time they'd brought her warm blankets and kept her covered. The staff seemed more caring, paying more attention to her, not like just another piece of meat.

"Maybe they've had a change in administration? The whole attitude's better." She was thinking like a person who'd run a retail shop. "Maybe they were just too busy the first time? Maybe they were understaffed?

"They sure asked a lot of questions. How many times do I have to tell them no allergies. Well, I'm glad they're being careful. I bet they're thinking about lawsuits. But they seemed like they actually cared. Nice.

"I hope I don't get stuck back out in the hall. That was awful last time. I hope I answered all the questions right. Is there anything I forgot to tell them?"

She was glad she wasn't having much pain; from them all asking her, she thought they must expect her to. Maybe she'd had enough pain medicine. She didn't want to be zonked out. But she could tell that the medicine wasn't helping her thinking any.

"Boy, I'm tired."

But here was Jessica again. "More forms, informed consent. I'll explain the procedure to you."

Jessica explained the surgery, including possible risks, death, paralysis, and all kinds of nasty and horrible things, not realizing that Alma wasn't listening. Alma was feeling the narcotic, and she was tired, and she was frustrated. Her mood was slipping. She was thinking, "This is a hospital; they're supposed to be helping me; this is starting to feel like torture."

But then she thought, "Oh, well, they're doing their job. I guess it's necessary. I guess. I hope they have a room for me soon, a warm one."

Her thoughts turned to an evening in her own warm house, and she and Brad discussing the book she was reading. She tried to remember the book but it wouldn't come to her. She remembered that they'd both liked it and they'd agreed on whatever issues it had brought up. Nice memories.

Jessica finally finished talking. Alma signed some papers, again with no idea what they were. In a different situation, she would've read them carefully before signing. And she would've checked out the hospital on the net and she could've checked out the doctor. But he seemed confident and Frank had endorsed him.

The information wouldn't have been too reassuring because the scores were average and the surgeon had some negative reviews. But she'd have realized that unsatisfied customers were more likely to post reviews than satisfied ones and that you couldn't please everyone. But Alma was in no position to do research, and her ignorance about things medical would've discouraged her from doing so or from understanding anything she read.

But that's all irrelevant, isn't it? Here she was, and here she would stay. She was in their hands and she might as well trust them. She didn't have the luxury of doing research and making choices.

She was alone in the trauma room again and she drifted off, to be awakened by Frank; maybe after fifteen minutes or it could've been two hours. There was a big clock on the wall but she hadn't been following it and she had no way to guess. Frank was enthused.

"Hey. We got a room. You ready?"

"Yes," she said, "I'm ready," and Frank and a new nurse wheeled her to the elevator. Two visitors in the elevator carefully stared straight ahead and two gaped at her with open curiosity, but Alma didn't care. She closed her eyes.

Once in her room, another nurse came in and the three hoisted her onto her bed, gently, causing minimal pain.

"There you go," said Frank. "You take care now."

Alma liked Frank. In situations like this, it's nice to have someone you feel some connection to, even as flimsy as this one, even for Alma.

"Thanks," said Alma, but Frank and one nurse had already wheeled the cart out of the room and scrammed before she'd had time to think.

The new nurse was young, plain, chubby, with no makeup but with a small silver ring in her right nostril which Alma, even in her state, noticed right away. She was dressed in street clothes, a relief after all the ER greens.

"Hi. Hope you're comfortable. Here's your buzzer if you need anything. I'm Sylvia, charge nurse on this floor. Your nurse will be Demonda; she'll be here in a while to take your vitals. I'm putting your clothes and stuff in the locker here; you'll want to keep it locked. I'll pin the key to your gown for now. Any valuables, you'll want to send them home with somebody or Demonda will give you a receipt and put them in the office safe. Any questions?"

"No, thank you," said Alma, who had barely followed anything the nurse had said. She closed her eyes.

"You look tired. After Demonda finishes, you can get some sleep. We'll take good care of you. OK?"

Alma promptly fell asleep. She woke up briefly when Demonda took her vital signs, asked about allergies and pain, adjusted her bedclothes and added another blanket. It wasn't as cold as in the ER but it wasn't as warm as Alma had hoped and she hadn't thawed yet. Demonda asked if she was comfortable and if she wanted to sleep now. By now the time, of which Alma was totally ignorant and in which she wasn't interested, was two ten in the afternoon. Demonda pulled down the shades and turned the lights down but not out. She showed Alma where the call button was pinned to her sheet, "Now you be sure and call for anything, anything at all. I'm pulling a double so I'll be back in around an hour and check on you again, vitals and all." She patted Alma on the shoulder and left, closing the door.

Due to the three PM change of shift, there was more noise in the corridor than usual but Alma was asleep as soon as the door clicked shut.

Alma spent three uneventful days in the hospital before surgery. She had occasional pain but she tried to avoid medication. Still, she did ask occasionally and so part of her day was passed in sleep. She got some books from a Pink Lady volunteer who came around with a book cart. They weren't great but she preferred reading to watching TV so she read, without much concentration or interest, and she couldn't have told you anything about what she'd read. Sometimes she'd remember some of the reading she and Brad had shared and the discussions they'd had. She really missed Brad although she'd been trying not to have feelings like that. "What's past is past. You can't change it and there's no point in dwelling on it." Alma couldn't have told you where she'd gotten that philosophy but she'd been good at sticking to it, at least until now.

The care was better than she'd expected. She'd heard some negative things about the hospital, particularly the nursing care. She remembered thinking that she hoped she'd never have to be a patient there and now she was. But her experience was positive. There were two nurses she didn't care for, but even those two seemed competent.

She didn't like the one she called "Miss WeWe."

"Well, how are we this morning?" "Did we have a nice lunch?" "Are we having any pain?"

And Miss WeWe was much more interested in casual conversation than Alma was. "Have you been watching the news? Wasn't that a terrible thing about the shooting? How could anybody do such a thing? They must've been crazy. Too bad they're dead. Maybe we could've learned something from them, why some people are like that."

Miss WeWe was annoying, but Alma didn't think it was worth the trouble to complain and she held back the sarcastic comments that ran through her head. After all, she was in the hands of Miss WeWe so it wouldn't be a good idea to piss her off, and they did seem competent hands, so Alma just smiled.

The other nurse she didn't care for was "The Grouch." As opposed to the sunshiny Miss WeWe, The Grouch always had a frown and was always in a hurry. She said little, just as well because what she did say was either brusque and professional, "I'll raise the head of your bed now. You're not getting up and moving enough," or negative, "Your bed is a mess this morning. I'll have to get someone to come straighten it out." Alma heard an accusatory tone in this. And with a swish of her skirts, being the only nurse Alma saw who wasn't wearing pants, she was gone. No inquiries about Alma and her well-being, again, unlike Miss WeWe. Alma figured she might have bad hemorrhoids or an unhappy love life, or both. Both of these ladies were taking care of her only until her surgery, so she didn't have to put up with them long; after surgery she'd be on a different floor. The rest of the nurses appeared competent and without irritating quirks. They were pleasant, seemed concerned, did their job and left.

Alma was surprised by visitors, two library clientele, three library staff, and Arnid and a waitperson from the coffee shop, seven during her first two days in the hospital. Alma didn't know how to react to them and they clearly didn't know how to interact with her. Each one asked about the hospital food, which Alma didn't really care about, as long as it was "Not bad." And most asked about the nursing care, "Pretty good, actually." Three asked about her injury and the surgery and her prognosis, which Alma thought intrusive and didn't care to discuss, but she politely shared a few general details rather than cutting them off. And three of them wanted to discuss their surgeries, which by some coincidence had all resulted in horror stories, and in that same hospital. Alma did cut those off, but politely, "Well, that sounds awful for you, gruesome. But tell me, what's new at the library?" or "Have you read anything interesting lately?"

Several visitors brought flowers, some attractive and some actually quite ugly. "Where do you go to buy ugly flowers?" Alma wondered to herself. She wasn't fond of flowers; she never bought them, but they did brighten up the room and she kept some of them. A couple of visitors brought candy, which Alma didn't want, but she left the boxes open near her bedside and offered it to the visitors and the nurses and it never lasted long.

Alma was also surprised that she felt touched by these visits rather than annoyed at the intrusions. She hadn't wanted visitors, and she didn't enjoy the visits, but still, she was touched.

She wondered how they knew she was there, but a visitor mentioned that one of the nurses was her boyfriend's sister. That explained it. Alma suspected there was something unethical, perhaps even illegal, about this lapse in confidentiality, but it was a minor matter. Then she realized she'd missed a shift at the library and hadn't thought to call. She was embarrassed; she'd never just missed a shift before. But clearly they knew her situation now and she didn't need to call to apologize.

Some of the visitors lingered. Alma soon learned to yawn. "Oh, excuse me. I am tired. The doctor said I need a lot of rest and not to visit too much. I really appreciate your coming, and thank you for the - flowers, or candy, or the book review magazine one had brought, the one gift Alma did appreciate.

She had a brief visit from Jessica, the ER nurse. Jessica asked, "How you doing?" and, "How are they treating you?" and "Is there anything you need? Anything I can do for you?"

Alma appreciated the visit; it hadn't felt like an intrusion. She wondered if this was just a courtesy or if Jessica actually was concerned that things maybe weren't being done properly on the floor, but Alma couldn't see any problems. She was grateful not to be cold anymore.

The day before surgery, Alma was tired of visitors. She asked her nurse to notify the front desk and to post a no visiting sign on her door, and so there were no more visitors, although she received a couple of silly cards and one more bouquet, actually quite attractive.

Then Frank, the ER blanketeer, came and sat down to visit. Jessica had stood but Frank didn't seem in a hurry. He asked the same questions as Jessica, and got the same answers, "I'm OK. It's fine." But then he asked, "Have they explained to you what's going on?"

"Well, they told me it's a bad break and I need surgery. It's tomorrow."

"That's all?"

"Yeah. What?"

Probably more had been explained in the ER, especially when she'd signed the surgical consent form, but she hadn't been listening and even if she'd listened, she couldn't have taken the information in while in that state, nor remembered it after.

"OK, you have a comminuted fracture, meaning your femur, your leg bone, is broken in two places so there's a piece floating loose there. It's not displaced; it's where it should be. The loose piece might not get enough blood and it could die, not good. There's jagged bone edges and a chance your artery there could get cut and you could bleed out, I mean people have bled to death right into their thigh. That's rare, but I've read about it. So they want the splint on and you not moving around until they fix it tomorrow. Clear?"

"I guess so," Alma said, but she thought she did understand; Frank's explanation had been clear. It wasn't scary; it sounded like it could be bad but that everything was under control.

"Is he a good surgeon?"

"Oh, yeah. He's the one I'd choose if it was me, God forbid." As soon as he said that, Frank thought it might've been insensitive. "Sorry," he said.

"That's OK. Thanks. Why was it so cold down there? Freezing. That's the main thing I remember. I think I'm only just thawed out."

Frank laughed. "Depends on who you ask. I've heard to keep germs down? To keep moisture from condensing on the instruments? To reduce bleeding? To keep visitors from staying too long? Gotta be someone higher up knows; it's way over my pay grade. It's gotta cost a fortune in air conditioning. There must be some good reason, but Jeez!"

"Jeez, indeed," replied Alma, who was enjoying the visit but getting tired. "Listen, thank you for coming. And especially for explaining. I appreciate it."

Frank got up. "No problem." Alma's lips tightened for a moment. She'd insisted that the wait staff at the coffee shop simply say "You're welcome," or "My pleasure," or some other simple appropriate response to a thank you. After all, why in the world should it be a problem to do the job you're being paid for? But this was a minor irritation and she was grateful to Frank who was now in the door. "OK, see ya. Take care now."

"Thanks, bye." And soon Alma was asleep again.

Just so you know, I tried to find out why the ER was so cold and like Frank, I got many different answers. Finally, an actual orthopedic surgeon explained that the staff was gowned up and working under hot bright lights, often masked, and they'd be uncomfortably hot if the ER and operating rooms weren't cold, maybe so uncomfortable that it could interfere with doing their job. Being a surgeon, he didn't mention the stress they worked under which I think could also contribute to their increased temperature, but surgeons generally are tough and don't attribute much to emotional stuff.

The three pre-op days weren't unpleasant, with the drowsing and reading, and even the visitors, and partly, again, because she didn't care much one way or the other about the food. But Alma was ready to get this over with.

The day of surgery, the surgeon popped in to say hello and that he'd be waiting for her in the OR, and not to worry, everything would be just fine. The anesthesiologist came next and introduced himself as the gas man. He explained what to expect in the operating room and in the recovery room. He asked if she was taking any medications, had any medical problems or any allergies.

Alma was used to these questions by now. No, she wasn't taking medications, vitamins, supplements. She wasn't against them; she'd just never needed them. She'd been getting her annual flu shot and she'd had her shingles vaccine, at the urging of Brad. He'd explained that the flu vaccine varied yearly in efficiency and was better than nothing. And that shingles was a leading cause of blindness in the elderly, which got Alma's attention. But medically speaking, that was it for her.

Alma had never been sick and she'd never had a pap smear or a mammogram. She'd been amazingly healthy, largely because she took good care of herself otherwise. You'd have expected more from an intelligent person, but she was willfully ignorant of medical things, medically illiterate you might say, and you can make some guesses as to the underlying reasons. And by the way, she also had never voted and had never been in a church service except for the three funerals. So now you're all caught up.

Alma noted that both the surgeon and the anesthesiologist were jocular in their approach, which she didn't find offensive but not reassuring either.

After the anesthesiologist left, her nurse came in. Demonda changed Alma's hospital gown and stuck a funny looking tissue paper hat on her, white with colored cartoon animals.

Demonda carefully removed the splint, shaved Alma's leg and sprayed it with antiseptic. She placed a pillow on each side of the leg. "Now listen up, this is important, the splint is off, so don't move that leg at all, not at all, got it?"

"Got it. Don't move," Alma replied.

Demonda started an IV and called in an aide, Mary Ellen, who we'll hear more of later. They carefully lifted Alma onto a cart.

Demonda patted Alma on the shoulder. "You take care now. Keep that leg still." Alma was starting to like Demonda.

Mary Ellen wheeled the cart out. "We're off to the operating room. Just relax and don't move."

Meanwhile, the surgical team was waiting in the cold operating room, the surgeon, the anesthesiologist, an assistant surgeon, a scrub nurse, a circulating nurse, and the surgical tech.

The anesthesiologist laughed. "She's a strange one," he said.

"How do you mean?" asked the surgeon.

"She doesn't seem afraid, nervous, at all, or at least she doesn't show it."

"Yeah, she's cool."

"I couldn't get her to laugh. I always get them to laugh, to help them relax a little. Not this one. Oh, and she's got no family, nobody in the waiting room."

"Nobody?"

"Nope, nobody."

"Sad," said the surgeon. "Well, I guess we're ready. How about some music?"

This was the tech's province. "Great, what's your poison?"

"I guess Beethoven for this one. Rock doesn't seem to fit her."

"You got it. She's a little old for rock." The tech put a CD in the player and Beethoven's Ode to Joy filled the room.

The surgeon answered, "I guess so, eighty, but she doesn't look it. You'd guess seventy at the most. She must take good care of herself. She's OK? Good to go?" he asked the anesthesiologist.

"Good to go. All the numbers are good. A healthy specimen. And really not bad looking, either."

"Oh, you noticed. Well, another day, another dollar. Let's get this show on the road."

The tech pushed the button to open the big OR door and stepped out. In a minute he and the aide wheeled Alma in. She immediately noticed that Ode to Joy was playing, one of Brad's favorites, although not hers. They'd listened to it together a few times, and she'd learned to appreciate it, a little. This memory made her feel both sad and comforted. She also noticed that the OR was frigid.

"Good morning, Alma," the surgeon greeted her. "You OK? You ready for this?"

"Yeah, I am if you are," she responded.

"I'm always ready," he replied.

Alma thought, "That's a little inappropriate. These surgeons."

"OK, Mary Ellen and this handsome young man are going to lift you onto this table. You don't do anything; let them do all the work, and the gas man here will have you count and you'll be asleep before you know it. Keep your leg still now."

The table was cold, but she suffered only briefly. The gas man attached a syringe to her IV tubing. "OK, this'll go in slow and you might feel a little tingly or a little burning, or get a bitter taste in your mouth. You ready?"

"Yeah, OK."

"Alright, here goes. Count backwards from ten and you'll be right asleep."

And she did, and she was, at four.

The surgery only took an hour and a quarter although the surgeon had told her it might take up to three hours. She didn't hear him pronounce, when he finished, "Excellent," or the assistant surgeon's, "Good job." And what happened later was probably not the surgeon's fault. Probably not.

Alma awoke confused, with a strange woman shaking her shoulder, "Alma. Alma. Wake up, honey. Alma."

Alma knew it wasn't her mother, who'd never called her anything but Mary Alma and never would've called her honey. She realized the woman must be a nurse.

"Surgery's over. It went fine. You're in the recovery room. I'm Cynthia. I'll be your nurse. You'll be here about an hour, and then we'll take you back to your room. Are you comfortable?"

"Thirsty."

"Of course. I'll get you some ice chips now and take your vital signs. If everything's OK in fifteen minutes, you can have some liquids and we have some nice sherbet if you want."

In fifteen minutes Alma was fine so she drank some water. The nurse brought a cup of orange sherbet and Alma slowly ate half of it. She said her throat was sore and Cynthia explained that she'd had a breathing tube down her throat. "You'll feel fine tomorrow. OK, I need to check on the lady next door. Be right back, but you just holler if you need anything. I'll hear you."

By the time she'd finished the sherbet, Cynthia was back. Alma's throat was already better; it hadn't been bad, just uncomfortable.

"Done with that? OK, they're here to take you to your room. They came early, want to get you in before shift change. Let me check your vitals again and then you're off." And she did and she was.

So far, so good?

WHAT HAPPENED AFTER ALMA'S SURGERY

Alma had barely settled in her new room and met her new nurse, "Charlotte. Call me Charlie. I'll be taking care of you," when Jessica, the ER nurse came in. Alma wasn't as surprised to see her this time. Jessica asked how she was doing and got the same responses as before, "Oh, I'm fine. Thanks for checking."

Alma never saw Jessica again.

She never saw the surgeon again either; he'd done his job and now she was in the hands of a hospitalist, an internal medicine specialist on the hospital staff.

Predictably, because of the kind of fracture, her age, and perhaps also because the hospital wasn't highly rated, Alma didn't do well after surgery. She got a fever and a cough and her chest hurt when she breathed. The nurses would quickly remind us that she didn't walk as much as they'd urged her to do, and they and the hospitalist blamed the pneumonia on her.

Alma wasn't severely ill. The IV antibiotic must've been an effective one because she got better surprisingly fast, except the cough wouldn't go away, but she wasn't bringing anything up after the third day.

The hospitalist was an older man, tall, lanky and balding, and always in a hurry. He listened to her chest every morning. He didn't talk much. Alma didn't like him and thought he was too old to still be working, although he was younger than she was. He told her the pneumonia was gone but she had to get up and walk more or she could get blood clots or even bed sores. He told her the lingering cough was common and would go away in a few days.

It didn't.

By the seventh day in the hospital, she was tired of it. She thought she was getting good care and she didn't have pain anymore but the Pink Lady didn't have many books that interested her when she felt well enough to read, and the nurses kept bugging her to walk even though walking hurt her leg. And after the pneumonia, she didn't have much energy and most of the time she refused. She was feeling harassed.

And she was lacking sleep. The hospital was noisy, day and night, with people walking and talking in the halls, and carts rolling by, squeaking and rattling, and worst of all, the speaker system - "Mary Ellen, come to the desk please." Mary Ellen, the nursing aide, was the most frequent target of the calls. Alma supposed she was hiding out in the stairwell smoking or something; they sure had trouble keeping track of her. And, "Doctor Benison, ICU please. Doctor Benison, ICU please." And the occasional "Code Blue, five south; Code Blue, five south." Alma didn't know what Code Blue meant, and she didn't ask, but she surmised that it wasn't anything good; else why would it be in code?

Alma thought they should turn the speaker system off at night so the patients could get some sleep. Couldn't they give the staff buzzers or pagers? Or surely they all had cell phones. She planned to write the administration about that after she got home.

And of course, they woke her in the middle of the night to check her vital signs, and they were drawing blood every other day which wasn't pleasant. And it was always cold.

But the day after the hospitalist pronounced her cured of pneumonia, her fever went up and her cough got worse, producing some ugly greenish stuff, and she was aching all over. She felt sick, really sick.

The nurse started an IV for another antibiotic, but after two days she wasn't any better and her leg was hurting again. The IV made it even harder to sleep and she rolled over on it and they had to restart it, in her other arm this time.

The hospitalist came in and for the first time, sat down to talk to her.

"You have Mersa; do you know what that is?"

"Never heard of it."

"It's M R S A, Methicillin-resistant Staphylococcus Aureus infection. It's bad because your cultures are resistant to all the antibiotics. It's very serious. Very serious. Do you understand?"

"How did I get that?"

"It's usually just in hospitals. We've had a few cases here. And getting the antibiotic for the pneumonia probably made you more susceptible."

"How do you treat it?"

"That's the thing. We don't have any good treatment; it's resistant. We can shoot in a mix of a lot of powerful antibiotics. That helps sometimes, but not often, and you might have some bad side effects. But it could work. The other option is to amputate your leg, that's where the MRSA infection seems to be, more than in your lungs, so far. But above-knee amputations are bad; it's harder to get a good prosthesis and they're harder to use. And of course, you'll still need antibiotics. But that's what we're recommending."

Alma frowned, and her mouth tightened. She said, "Well, there's a third option."

"Third option? No, I don't think so. What's that?"

"We don't do anything."

"No, you don't understand. You'll die. You'll die if we don't do something."

"Yes, I do understand. That's OK. I'm not having any amputation and the antibiotics sound like a waste of time and money."

"But you'll die."

"Yeah. That's what you told me. Now, if you don't have anything else?" Alma was telling him to leave, but he misunderstood.

"No, no, there's nothing else. The antibiotics, and best with the amputation. There's nothing else."

"OK, I think we're done. Tell the nurse to take out this IV please; I'm sick of it." Alma was feeling very tired.

"Look, you need to think about it. You can't stay in the hospital; your insurance won't cover it if you're not getting treatment."

"No problem. I'll take care of it." She saw the need to be more direct, although still not rude or crude. "You can go now."

Alma had health insurance when she worked full-time in the dress shop. When she bought the coffee shop, Arnid persuaded her to sign onto the plan she gave the employees; she still had that. Of course, the bill was going to be astronomical, but if the insurance wouldn't pay she had plenty of money. That wouldn't be a problem.

The hospitalist stood up, an ugly frown on his face. "OK. OK, you think about it. I'll be back tomorrow and we'll talk about it."

"No, I don't think so. You don't need to come back. Thank you anyway."

The hospitalist left, shaking his head in an exaggerated fashion because he wanted Alma to see it and get the message.

Alma thought she might go home and hire nurses to take care of her while she waited to die, assuming the hospitalist's assessment was accurate. She had the fleeting thought, "Maybe they push amputations just to make more money," but she decided this was being too wary. If she really was going to die from this, she didn't want to die in her house. And even though she disliked the hospital, it'd be a hassle getting transportation and managing the nurses. It'd be simpler just to stay where she was and let things slide.

Charlie came in. "Are you sure you want to stop this IV? That's what Doctor said, but are you sure?"

"Yes, I'm sure. Please get this thing off of me."

"Well, it's running good. Maybe you'd like to keep it `til tomorrow and then decide? You wouldn't need to have one re-started if you change your mind."

"I won't change my mind. I don't do that. Take it out, please."

"OK, then." Charlie was deft and it was already out, no pain, no problem. "I'm really sorry."

Alma recognized from Charlie's face and her voice that she genuinely was sorry, not just saying it. Alma just nodded, and Charlie left.

In the expectable course of things, Alma's left lung stopped functioning. It was hard to breathe and quite uncomfortable. They gave her oxygen through a cannula under her nose and that helped a bit. Her blood pressure dropped and they gave her medicine to keep it up. The hospitalist and some of the nurses kept urging her to let them start an IV for medicine, but she refused. She finally had to get rude and crude to get the hospitalist to drop it. She didn't regret that; she thought he'd had it coming for a while. Her kidneys begin to shut down, her heartbeat became irregular, and anybody who knew anything could tell she was dying. Alma herself could tell she was dying, she being, of course, nobody's fool.

Alma noticed she wasn't getting the attention she had been. Her assigned nurses checked her vital signs once a shift and they still answered if she buzzed, still promptly, usually, but they weren't making the occasional drop-in, "How you doing?" visits they had before. And the hospitalist, she never did get his name and she never liked him, still came once a day, but he had been spending ten or fifteen minutes in her room before and now he was in and out in about two, facilitated by Alma's unwillingness to engage in conversation with him.

The next day, two chaplains visited, an older Catholic priest and later a younger protestant. She took their visits as an ominous sign and quickly chased each of them away without resorting to rudeness or crudeness although she had to be forceful with the younger one, who had evangelical leanings and was intent on enquiring into the state of her soul.

That afternoon the two chaplains had their weekly meeting over coffee in the cafeteria. The coffee was pretty bad, but they were used to it. The priest had been at the hospital for years and was mentor of the younger man, who'd recently been hired after finishing his internship elsewhere. They weren't aware that he wouldn't last long, due to complaints from patients and their families.

He was addressing his mentor. "I don't know what happened. I tried my best."

"You tried your best to do what?" The priest was already familiar with the younger's approach

"To save her soul. I think she's dying."

"Did she want her soul saved?"

"No, that's it. She obviously didn't. So it's kind of urgent if she's dying."

"Tell me about the conversation, from the beginning."

"That'll be easy. It wasn't very long." The younger man related the conversation.

The priest frowned. "OK. What do you think the problem was?"

"Well, Satan is about in the world, and in this hospital. Her heart was hardened and I couldn't get through to her. Why would she be like that?" asked the younger, apparently forgetting what he'd just said about Satan.

The priest took a sip of coffee. "You know, so much of our religion doesn't really make sense. It has to be looked at with an open heart, and some people are just up in their heads. And some have been burned by the church or by some 'Christian,' and they don't understand that those are human things, so they turn against God. And some fear being dependent, and that's what God offers us, isn't it? So they use their anger or their intellect to ward Him off. It's sad."

The younger man had stopped listening halfway through this. He didn't think highly of his mentor and felt he had little to offer. He'd learned little from the older man so far, and didn't think he would learn much more in the future. Neither did his mentor.

"There you go again, psychology stuff. That's too deep for me. I think it's just Satan's work."

The priest actually had doubts about the existence of Satan. He had doubts about a lot of things. But he also had certainties. He was sure of God's love for us all, so he had doubts about Hell. He thought maybe it wasn't a place but a state of separation from God. He was a man of faith who continually struggled with his faith.

The younger man wasn't troubled by doubts or uncertainties. As you saw, if he started to slip into wondering instead of knowing, he quickly redirected his thinking. This ability was one of the few things he and Alma had in common.

The older man spoke again, "Do you think you were pressuring her?"

"Of course I was pressuring her."

"How well did that work?"

"Look, she needs to understand the Gospel. That's what I was explaining to her."

"In my experience, when you pressure people, they usually just put up more resistance. You need to be clear about your goal and then choose the approach that'll most likely lead there."

The young chaplain dismissed this. "Well, I know we don't share the same beliefs. I hate to think of her burning in Hell for eternity. I'd hate to think I hadn't done everything I could to save her."

"Could you imagine that maybe it's not up to you to save her? Anyway, you might want to rethink your approach a bit."

The young man was certain again. "I don't have any choice. May God have mercy on her soul."

The priest pushed his half-finished lukewarm cup of coffee aside and stood up. "Well, on that we agree. Let's continue to pray for her." He moved away from the table. He felt he was having no more success with the young man than the young man was having with Alma. He recalled what Tom Paine said, "Trying to convince someone whose mind is made up is like trying to give medicine to a dead man."

Once out of the young man's sight, he crossed himself. Sometimes he thought he'd been in this job too long, but he couldn't imagine anything he'd rather be doing.

Meanwhile, back on the floor, Alma buzzed and Charlie came in. She looked tired.

"Is there something I can do for you?"

Alma was thinking, "Well, would I have buzzed if there wasn't?" but she only said, "Yeah. First, please turn off this darn machine; that beeping's getting on my nerves and I'd like some peace and quiet."

"Oh, I can't do that."

"Why not?"

"Well, that's monitoring your heartbeat. That's what it's for."

"And why would we be doing that?" Alma asked.

"Well, to monitor your heart."

"Look. I'm DN, that leave me alone thing. So what does it matter?"

"DNR?"

"Yeah. DNR; don't do nothing. So you don't need to monitor my heart cause you're not gonna do anything anyway, right?"

"Umm. I guess so. I'll have to ask the doctor. Anything else?"

Charlie appeared to be trying to stop herself, with difficulty, from backing out of the room.

"Yeah. It's so cold in here. Can you turn up the heat?"

"Sorry; it's set for the whole floor, not for the rooms. I'll have them bring you some more blankets. OK, you take care now."

She was nearly out of the room now.

"Just a minute. Blankets would be very nice. One more thing. I want to see Frank."

"Frank?"

"That nice young nurse from downstairs, Frank."

"Oh, Frank from the ER. OK, I'll see if he's on and if he can come see you. And I'll send the blankets. You take care now." And she was gone.

Later that afternoon, Frank showed up. "Hey, how you doing?"

"Depends on how you look at it I guess," Alma replied. "Could you sit down for a minute? You look tired."

"Yeah, sure, I got a minute. I'm pulling another double. On my break now. We're short-staffed and we're all doing doubles."

"Oh, I'm sorry. That's too bad. Thank you for coming. I won't keep you long."

"That's OK, glad to do it, nice to see you again."

"Well. I don't know about that, the shape I'm in. But I appreciate you coming. Will you do something else for me?"

"If I can. I'm not authorized on this floor. I can't get you blankets or anything but I can ask them out there for you."

"No, they said they're coming with the blankets. That's not the thing. This'll sound funny, but could you hold my hand for a little while?"

"Hold your hand? Sure, I can do that. Glad to." Frank pulled his chair closer to the bed, took Alma's hand in his, and then put his other hand on top. His hands were nice and warm; Alma's were not.

"How's this?"

"Fine. That's just what I wanted."

They were silent for several minutes. Frank was thinking, "They don't teach this in nursing school." But Frank was a natural, and some things you can't really teach.

Alma was wondering why she wanted someone to hold her hand, but she thought that given her age and condition, she was entitled to it if that's what she wanted; she wasn't going to worry about it. And if she did want her hand held, who better than Frank? Especially considering how limited the possibilities were.

Frank said, "You're not delirious."

"Delirious?"

"You know, out of your head. Happens a lot in the hospital, especially post-op, especially with fever and infection and all." He carefully left out, `or dying.' "Charlie thought you might be getting delirious when you asked for me."

"No. I'm not at my best, but I'm not out of my head. Never have been, as far as I know."

"Are you afraid?"

"No. Nothing to be afraid of. I guess I'm just a little bit lonely."

"Have you had visitors?"

"No. I was surprised when some came at first, but then I didn't want any more. They were uncomfortable and they made me uncomfortable. They were mostly a nuisance."

"Yeah, I can see that, I guess. But you wanted me to hold your hand for while."

"Yeah, I appreciate it. That's enough now. I don't wanta take up any more of your time."

"It's OK. No problem."

"Don't say that, please. You're tired and this is your break. It is a problem. Just say, `You're welcome.' OK?"

"OK. You're welcome then. I'll go now. I'll come back tomorrow if I can. I'm on another double."

"That's nice. You did what I needed today. Thanks. You take care now."

"You too."

Alma was thinking, "He won't need to come tomorrow; I don't think I'll be here." She was also thinking how much she liked Frank, and that she wished they'd hurry up with the blankets.

After Frank left, Alma thought up a joke. "I'm three months over eighty years old, and that should be enough. Too much of a good thing can kill you." She chortled to herself. One of the aides in the hall heard her chortle and thought she must be delirious, but she wasn't.

But Alma was still there the next day after all; she'd been taking care of herself for years and she was tougher and in better shape than anyone could've imagined. Frank wasn't able to get back, although he hadn't forgotten. Some days the ER was just swamped.

Alma got more uncomfortable. The hospitalist ordered a full oxygen mask and that helped some. He finally convinced Alma to allow another IV, not for antibiotics but for fluids and some medicine to make her more comfortable. He wasn't a warm and fuzzy guy, but he wasn't unkind.

That afternoon, Alma buzzed and an aide she didn't know came in, after a while.

"Can I help you?"

"You sure can. Get me Charlie."

"Charlie's pretty busy now. What can I do for you?"

"I told you. You can get me Charlie."

The aide, who was also pulling doubles and was worrying about her home situation and her finances, got a little short.

"And I told you, she's busy."

"One more time, get me Charlie. I can get up and go find her but I don't feel like it. Do I need to call the hospital administrator? Charlie!" Alma, with the help of the oxygen, still had enough breath to speak up forcefully but her yell didn't carry far.

"OK, OK. I'll tell her."

"Thank you very much."

"No problem," the aide said, either sarcastically or just out of habit, and left the room.

Either way, Alma thought, "Oh, shit."

Charlie came in soon. "Sorry, I was in a meeting but I escaped. What's going on?"

"I want this IV out."

Charlie put her stethoscope in her ears. "Let me listen to your chest."

You might be wondering why Charlie listened to Alma's chest at this point. Or maybe you didn't wonder; anyway, I did. Was it a way to show authority? Or maybe she was just curious. Or it could be because medical professionals always have to *do something,* not just stand there feeling futile, helpless, and useless. Anyway, she listened and she didn't like what she heard.

Charlie removed the stethoscope from her ears and pulled Alma's bedclothes back up to her neck. "You want the IV stopped," she said.

"Yes, and please turn up the oxygen." Alma was feeling very tired.

"OK, I can do that. I'll have to call the doctor about the IV."

"Do that please. Now," Alma said.

Charlie was back in a few minutes and took out the IV. "OK," she said, "OK?"

Alma sighed and nodded.

Charlie stood looking at her for a moment, and then Alma was startled when Charlie stooped and kissed her on the forehead. Then she quickly turned and left. Alma watched the door close behind her.

Alma had long believed that dwelling on the past was a waste of time and energy and just led to unnecessary pain. But she couldn't help reflecting on her life during the last hours of it. She took an inventory.

She'd never had children, nor ever wanted any; raising her siblings when she was a child was quite enough for her, thank you very much.

She hadn't traveled, except for her two cruises, and she'd never had any urge to do more.

She'd become knowledgeable in many fields and she'd gotten satisfaction from her learning and from helping some people, who like her, had grown through their reading, books she'd selected for them.

She'd had two rewarding relationships, not even counting Hank, although the last one was much too brief. She wasn't sure if she'd ever experienced love, loving someone else, but with Brad there'd been something close to it, and that was enough

Although she couldn't put it into words, she had some awareness that she'd become less wary and controlling and she was glad she'd made progress on that before she met Brad.

She'd suffered losses, but, "That's just life," and she'd survived them.

She'd reached, indeed, surpassed, her goals of making a lot of money and being independent

Then Alma had the thought that in her whole life, she'd never said the L word to another human being. She thought, "Well, maybe it's not too late. I could call Charlie in and tell her." She chuckled. "Then they really would say I'm delirious."

And then, in her final lucid moments, before she slipped off with Brad and Grandma Alma and the two angels who were all patiently waiting to guide her through the tunnel of light, Alma's last thought was that her life hadn't been bad, really, not bad at all.

ACKNOWLEDGMENTS

Enormous gratitude to Chris Thomas, writing coach extraordinaire, who deserves enormous credit for this book's existence. Any blame goes to me.

Thanks to the special editors, Steve Reed, Tom Woodward, Victor Whitman, and Annette Kazmerski, for the huge amount of work they gave to this.

And to Martha Puryear, of course.

And to the other valuable readers and advisers, Doris Allen, Laura Carthy, Michael Ginsberg, Betsy Maxon, Wynne Snoots, Robb Thompson, Karolyn Wayman, Robb Wilson and Ron Yoder.

To others who have been so helpful, Sister Paula and all the sisters, Dr. Jake and Jerri Poff.

Also thanks and many apologies to anyone I've left out. Sorry.

Thank You All!

ABOUT THE AUTHOR

Doug Puryear is a retired psychiatrist living in Santa Fe, NM, with his long term wife, a keeper. He enjoys writing, playing the guitar, and fly fishing, and especially his family. This is his seventh book and first novel.

He maintains a blog at addadultstrategies.wordpress.com.

He hopes you enjoyed the book, and he'd appreciate your posting a review on one of the book selling websites.

You can find all of his books listed there by searching "Douglas Puryear."

Printed in Great Britain
by Amazon